INTRODU
JEMIMA
FEATS
OF TRUE
BALANCE

Also by Phil Earle

Storey Street

Demolition Dad

Superhero Street

For older readers

Being Billy

Saving Daisy

Heroic

Bubble Wrap Boy

For younger readers

Albert and the Garden of Doom

Elsie and the Magic Biscuit Tin

Phil Earle

The War Next Door

Illustrated by Sara Ogilvie

Orion
Children's Books

ORION CHILDREN'S BOOKS

First published in Great Britain in 2016 by Hodder and Stoughton

1 3 5 7 9 10 8 6 4 2

A CIP catalogue record for this book is available from the British Library.

ISBN 978 1 4440 1391 7

Printed and bound in Great Britain by Clays Ltd, St Ives plc

The paper and board used in this book are from well-managed forests and other responsible sources.

MIX
Paper from responsible sources
FSC® C104740

Orion Children's Books
An imprint of
Hachette Children's Group
Part of Hodder and Stoughton
Carmelite House
50 Victoria Embankment
London EC4Y 0DZ

An Hachette UK Company
www.hachette.co.uk

www.philearle.com
@philearle
www.facebook.com/PhilEarleAuthor
www.hachettechildrens.co.uk

This book is dedicated to my friend, Matthew Williams, who spotted that the house had been stolen in the first place, and to my brother Bob, Milner by name, but never by nature.

P.E.

For Eve, Ian, Rowan & Gil

S.O.

FLOSS LIVES HERE
JAKE LIVES HERE
MASHERS HOUSE
THE HOUSE THAT WAS STOLEN
DANNYS HOUSE
Welcome to Storey Stre

SCHOOL
MOUSE LIVES HERE
CURL UP and DYE
25/7 CORNER SHOP
WOKEVER YOU WANT
OH MY COD
THE STAGGER INN
PULSE'S FUNERAL

Who's Who in Storey Street...

The Z-List:

Jeremiah

Jacqueline

John-boy

Naughty, Naughty

Stealing is bad, kids.

Naughty.

Devious.

The sort of behaviour that is frowned upon with a tut-tut and a brow more wrinkled than a sun-kissed raisin.

But let's face it, some stealing is worse than others.

I mean, pinching a biscuit from the tin when your mum's back is turned is hardly the sort of thing that deserves ten years hard labour. And 'borrowing' a particularly hard answer from the smart kid next to you in a maths test doesn't mean you should be exiled to a mountain prison and made to break rocks with your own forehead.

That said, there are certain things you should never pinch, like someone's bum when they're not expecting it, and there are others

that you simply can't. I've never heard of anyone successfully shoplifting a rhinoceros by hiding it up their jumper, or making a whole country disappear using just the rubber on the end of their pencil.

I did once, though, hear about a house that was stolen.

Don't roll your eyes at me. It's a strange tale, but true. In fact, when it happened it almost started a war, a war like no other.

You see, this house was special. So special that this wasn't even the first time it had been stolen. And I don't mean burgled. Anyone can be unlucky enough to have their belongings nicked by a stinking rotter with a swag bag and a mask.

What I mean is that this house had been properly stolen, twice: the bricks, the door, the roof . . . everything!

Don't look at me like I'm a loon, and don't throw this book on the fire, either. I know it sounds weird, but I promise you it happened.

This is the story of how The House That Was Stolen was stolen.

So settle back, open your mind really wide, and let the battle begin . . .

At Home with the Milners

It was a sunny morning on Storey Street.

Birds sang, badgers danced, and foxes picked the pockets of any dustbins left recklessly overflowing.

At Number 29, it was business as usual.

Coffee brewed, toast browned, while on the floor, two figures wrestled to the death. Well, not quite to the death, but with enough aggression to make a trip to the hospital highly likely.

'Submit!' the larger figure yelled, the sleeves of his crisp, white shirt rolled up to reveal arms the size of Russia.

From underneath this hulking, but impeccably dressed figure, came a defiant noise.

'Never!' it yelled happily, despite its mouth being pushed into the floor. 'You'll have to rip my arms out of the sockets before I give in!'

The larger figure laughed. 'Who'll clean my shoes if I do that?!'

Still he didn't let go, instead twisting the smaller figure's arm further behind his back, before demanding, 'SUBMIT!' again.

What happened next beggared belief. Somehow, despite being three times lighter, the smaller figure managed to push himself first onto his hands and knees, then into a crouch, until finally, with sweat pouring off his shaven skull, Masher Milner stood beside his dad, Maurice, snarling like a Rottweiler with a toothache. What a fearsome pair they were. The scariest, most cunning bad boys, not only on Storey Street, but in the whole of Seacross.

'I'll never submit!' Masher laughed, despite the effort and pain. 'So get used to it, Dad. The next person to give in will be you!'

Well, that sort of challenge was enough to kick Maurice and Masher Milner into a new level of warfare. Across the kitchen table they tumbled, scattering plates and cutlery, leaving buttery slices of toast stuck to the seats of their trousers.

Not that either of them noticed, or even cared. They were so caught up in their fight that they could've covered themselves in porridge and neither would've paused to lick their lips. Only the arrival of a third person in the kitchen brought them back to their senses, as the shrill shriek of a hearing aid threatened to shatter every glass they owned into a squillion pieces.

'Masher!! Maurice!! How many times do I have to tell you? If you want to fight, do it in the garden like the other wild animals. Your granddad would turn in his grave if he could see the mess in here.'

Tentatively, Masher lifted his head to look at the trail of devastation behind them, not to mention the craggy scowl of his grandmother, Lillian. She may have only stood four feet tall in her wrinkly-stockinged feet, but he knew better than to incur her wrath. Others had done so and disappeared. (Granddad included.)

She had every right to be irked. There was cream on the walls, orange juice on the windows, and unless Masher was mistaken, half a packet of Frosties stuck to the ceiling with marmalade. Modern art, it wasn't. Carnage, it was.

'Don't you be worrying, Ma,' Maurice said as he pushed himself up off the floor. 'Our Quentin will tidy it up, won't you, son?' And he flicked a globule of strawberry jam, which landed on the boy's forehead.

Masher grimaced, and not just at the jam that was oozing into his eye. He hated it when his dad used his real name. He only did it to wind him up. Dad knew his true name wasn't Que— (He didn't even like saying it in his own head.)

His name was Masher.

It summed him up, physically and mentally. Mashing was what he did, to everyone and everything.

And he did it bloomin' well. Everyone said so, especially his teachers. So when Dad called him by that other abomination of a name, it made him want to scream.

What kind of parent gives their son such a woofer of a name anyway?

Well, let me tell you. Maurice was the worst kind of person, and not only because he was an estate agent.

OK, he did make his money selling rubbish houses that were held together with double-sided sticky tape, but that wasn't the worst thing about him.

No, what made him really smell of rotten chicken livers was the fact that he was also a snob.

A hoity-toity, nose in the air, looks-at-you-like-you're-dog-dooon-his-polished-shoe snob.

He hated anyone with less money than him, and he didn't like rich people either. Because rich people had money that should really belong to him.

But not for long. Not if Maurice had it his way. He had plans, and all of them were more snobby than a traffic jam full of Rolls-Royces.

Reluctantly, Masher fell to his knees and began scraping Frosties into a pile, while his dad poured a steaming cup of tea.

'How many houses are you planning on selling today, Maurice?' Lillian asked.

'At least a couple,' Maurice bragged through a mouthful of toast.

'Two? Is that all? When your dear old dad had his grocer's shop he had to re-stock it fifteen times before lunch alone. '

Masher watched Dad roll his eyes and tried to remember how many times he'd heard his grandma say that. He'd run out of fingers and toes to count about seven years ago, and had run the batteries down on several calculators since.

Dad pushed himself to his feet and smiled thinly at his beloved, irritating mother.

'Now, now, my precious. I may only be selling two houses

today, but they happen to have seven bedrooms each. By the time the suckers sign on the dotted line, I'll be owed so much dosh the Bank of England will have to open a new money-printing factory. One they'll name after me. In fact, they'll have to take the Queen off the fifty-quid note and stick me on it instead!'

Masher chuckled to himself, imagining how it would feel to have his face on a note too. The ten-pound note to his dad's fifty. How great it would be to walk into a shop and buy himself a new pair of boots with steel toecaps, using cash with his own mush on it. Everyone would know just how rich and important his family was.

Just as his blissful daydream was gathering pace, Masher heard a familiar thud against the wall behind him. Then another. And another. Again and again.

Masher felt his temperature rise and his hands curl into fists. Across the kitchen, his dad was reacting the very same way. Only Grandma was oblivious, her hearing aid needing new batteries again.

'You are kidding me!' Masher grunted.

'At this time of the morning?' Dad replied.

Masher stormed out of the kitchen. 'Why don't you let me handle this?' he said over his shoulder.

By the time Milner Jnr reached the front door, he was primed, ready and in full-on Mashing mode. It was a sight scary enough to have the Incredible Hulk screaming for his teddy.

'Watch me, Dad,' he growled. 'Watch. Me. Mash!'

3.

The Family Next Door

Neighbours. Everybody needs good neighbours.

I'm sure that's a line from the Bible. Or did I see it on the telly? Oh, I don't know – either way it's true. There's nothing better than sharing a wall with people who like a laugh and a joke; friends you can grow old with, comparing denture cream and surgical stockings. You know, the important things in life.

Imagine living next door to the Milners, though. You've only had one chapter of their hoity-toitiness, but I can't imagine you'd dare hang your Y-fronts out to dry with them sneering over the garden fence. Who would?

It seems fitting, then, that Masher and his family only had one set of direct neighbours, the Catt family, who lived on their left.

The Catts were so terrified of the Milners that they never went out of their house unless absolutely necessary. The curtains never opened, the front step was never scrubbed, the cobwebs were so huge that the spiders had spun a double garage and a conservatory on the side. Such was the family's fear, the local kids had named them 'The Scaredy Catts'. Never was a nickname more apt. Well, apart from Quentin Milner's.

The house on the other side of Milner Mansions was . . . well . . . how do I describe it? It was a house like no other, mainly because it wasn't a house at all. Except it was. Kind of. Confused? Me too. Let me try and explain.

The House That Was Stolen had been there for ever. At least, we think it had. Official records of its history and ownership had mysteriously disappeared just after the Second World War.

The House That Was Stolen was simply a gap, a void in the shape of a house, which sat between the Milners' abode and the one belonging to the Christmas family. To the untrained eye, it looked like a sneaky burglar had whipped the house away, brick by brick, overnight. But instead of leaving no trace at all, this thief had left behind three things: a settee, a TV and a lamp, which sat where the living room should have been.

No one knew how or why these objects were there. It had been that way for as long as people could remember.

There were legends about how it all started. That the tooth fairy set it up as a crash pad as she twinkled her way across the country, sliding pound coins under pillows. That it was some kind of art that was meant to be all profound but just looked a bit . . . rubbish.

Either way, you can imagine how this annoyed the Milners, can't you? There they were, with curtains sewn by their own enslaved silkworms and an eighty-carat gold doorknocker (well, almost), only to live next door to what looked like an open-air charity shop.

They'd tried endlessly to have the furniture removed, bombarding the council with emails until harassed workers came to take the stuff away.

But the weird thing was, no matter how many times the site was cleared, the next morning, the same items reappeared: a settee, a TV and a lamp.

How odd, and utterly, utterly wonderful. I mean, what kind of mischievous, impish, talented and handsome person would do such a thing . . . ?

Well, after years and years of trying, the Milners finally gave up, though the failure left its mark on Masher and his dad. They were uber-sensitive to anything and everything that went on there. A dog whistle being blown from The House That Was Stolen was enough to have them snarling and barking out of their windows.

The House That Was Stolen was a landmark on the road, more important to the residents than Number 10 was to the folk of Downing Street.

It was especially important to the kids who lived on Storey Street, who had adopted the space as their own; a place where they could escape their parents, kick back with friends and pretend to watch TV. Summer or winter, there was always someone occupying the settee, reading by the 'light' of the lamp. In fact, that constituted a quiet day at The House. All sorts of events were held there: impromptu art exhibitions, card schools, squash tournaments, acoustic music gigs. Moira and Marvin Marshall had met there at the age of eight, the latter proposing on the settee ten years later. And with that sort of history, there was only ever going to be one venue for the wedding, which saw a hundred people cramming into the tiny space, dancing the night away.

This morning was a little more sedate, but certainly not quiet, despite it only being eight o'clock. The bright sunshine had dragged the children of Storey Street from their beds like moths to a flame. (Not that anyone's getting burned here, honest. It's not that kind of story. It's just a simile.)

On the settee, Polly Stagger, Anaya Shan and Eleanor Pulse

were debating the merits of Justin Bieber's new single (it was a very short debate), while next to them tutted Laszlo Di Bosco, who was watching the telly. (Poor lad never had grasped the concept of electricity.)

Behind them was where the real action was, though. A game of three-a-side footie had kicked off, with the Storey Street Trophy (a highly polished old tin of beans) at stake.

Leading the two teams were Elliot Tipps (son of legendary Seacross City Tigers goalkeeper, Tony Tipps) and hapless Danny Christmas (son of the local vicar, who lived on the other side of The House That Was Stolen).

Danny's dad had been a vicar for as long as Danny could remember, a job that caused him no end of pain at school. Not because of his dad's unshakeable beliefs – none of the kids batted an eyelid at those. Danny found himself the butt of so many jokes

because of Dad's name.

You see, the surname Christmas, plus a job as a vicar made Danny's dad . . . FATHER CHRISTMAS.

I know that shouldn't be funny snort . . . but it doesn't matter how many times I hear it . . . giggle . . . it still tickles me . . . guffaw.

Danny was an enthusiastic footballer, but limited in ability. While a lot of poor players seem to have two left feet, it was as if Danny had twelve, and managed to trip over them every minute.

This morning, he found himself in goal, for which the posts were drawn in chalk on the Milners' kitchen wall. In the ten minutes they'd been playing, he'd already let in seventeen goals, each one a rocket from Elliot's left boot. It was this repeated sound of leather on brick that had Masher and his dad bolting from their house like a pair of rabbits who'd spotted a ten-metre carrot.

'Oi! Rudolph!' Masher boomed in Danny's direction. This was one of a number of hilarious Christmas-themed insults Masher regularly threw at his neighbour. 'Elf' and 'Cracker' were other favourites, though none stuck as firm as 'Rudolph' – helped by the fact that, all year round, Danny's nose was as red as a baboon's bum.

Masher saw panic flare in his prey's eyes, and felt a surge of pride at his power.

'What do you want me to burst first – your ball or that zit you call a nose?'

Danny instinctively covered his face, which unfortunately didn't leave enough hands to shove the ball up his jumper. He'd already lost three that month to Masher, and he couldn't afford another.

'It's not my fault,' whimpered Danny. 'Blame Elliot. Someone's hidden dynamite in his boots . . . and it wasn't me!'

But Masher wasn't about to turn his attentions away from Danny. Not when he enjoyed terrorising him so.

'Now listen here, bauble bonk,' Masher growled. 'My dad and me were in the middle of something important. But we can't concentrate because of them leaky buckets you call hands . . .'

Danny looked glumly at his fingers, red and sore from trying to stop Elliot's shots. He was worried Masher was going to make things worse by snapping them off, one by one.

'. . . So you've got one option: STOP! IMMEDIATELY! Or I'll tie you up in tinsel and strap you to that manky lamp. Understand?!'

Danny understood perfectly. He made it his business to listen very carefully when Masher spoke. Living almost next door to him was a daily, painful nightmare.

'I'll stop, immediately,' Danny sighed, to the groans of the other players.

'But we've only just started,' said Elliot.

'And anyway,' piped up another lad, little Jack Boo, who for some ridiculous reason was feeling brave. 'It's not like you own this pitch. We've been playing here for years. My dad did too when he was little. And my granddad, and his dad t—'

'ENOUGH!' bellowed Masher. 'I don't care if this crummy piece of land belongs to the king of Switzerland. I'm telling you to get off it. Before I open the can of whoop-ass I have in my pocket.'

The boys gulped and looked to Masher's pocket, but all they could see was the top of a blunt pencil and a bloodied tissue. Regardless, it was enough to have them bricking it. The final whistle had blown and Masher had won, three hundred-nil. Glumly, they plodded away, but not before the bully had grabbed the ball and reduced it to a pancake.

'Did you see, Dad? I showed them who's boss, didn't I?' Masher said eagerly when he went back inside.

'You did, son,' answered Maurice, who seemed distracted.

With a satisfied grin, Masher turned his attention to the deflated ball, ripping it into a dozen leather strips before tying one of them, warrior-like, around his forehead.

It might not have been a crown, and his subjects might not like him, but he still felt like a king.

Location, Location, Location

Masher was no expert, but the house in front of him seemed to resemble a palace. It was as if Cinderella had shoved her dream castle on the back of a lorry and shipped it to the middle of Seacross. Why she'd want to live there he had no idea, but he couldn't help being impressed.

It wasn't Cinderella's palace, of course. Everyone knew that she and Charlie Charming had built a smashing place just outside of Grimsby. No, this palace was the brainchild of Maurice Milner. And how proud he was of it, too.

'You really built this place, Dad?' Masher asked, as his eyes scanned all five storeys.

'Sort of. It was a double garage when we bought it. Only had three walls and half a ceiling, but the rats didn't mind. Hundreds of them there were, like a living carpet, scurrying around the place.'

'Well, there's no sign of them now,' Masher said. 'It's too posh for the Queen's corgis, never mind rats. Looks like it cost a fortune!'

This seemed to please Dad, who ushered Masher inside.

'Appearances can be deceiving, son – an illusion,' he said slyly. 'And I'm the best magician in the world. Take that wall, for instance. Look at it – rock steady.'

Masher stared. It was a big wall, the sort that looked as if it supported the rest of the house.

'A wall that size would cost a fair bit in bricks and mortar. And the only fortune I'm interested in is my own. So I didn't use normal bricks, did I?'

'What did you use, Dad?' Masher asked. There was nothing that looked different about it.

'Lego, son.' Maurice looked as smug as a man who'd just invented a hair-cutting hat.

'Lego? But those bricks are tiny. That'd cost a mint!'

'Oh, I didn't *buy* them. Don't be a wally. I've a network of contacts who work in kids' nurseries. Once the little darlings have gone home they fill their bags and bring 'em to me. I pay out a few quid, they're happy, and within a month I've enough for a wall or two.'

'But why isn't that wall multi-coloured like Lego?'

'I covered it, didn't I?'

'In wallpaper?'

Maurice shook his head. 'Toilet roll. It's way cheaper. Bit of paint on top of that quilted stuff and it looks top drawer. For long enough anyway.'

'And is Lego strong enough to support the rest of the house?'

'What do you reckon?' Maurice looked over his shoulder, before whispering, ''Course it isn't. But I'm going to sell it so quick that by the time the new owners realise, it'll be too late. It'll be their responsibility.'

'Won't they know you renovated it too?'

Maurice smiled. 'Nope. If they try to find the builder, they'll hit seventeen dead ends and phantom companies, before giving up. When you're as powerful as me, my boy, you can keep your name off the books. All I'm doing, as far as the owners are concerned, is selling the place. Come on. I'll show you the rest.'

Up endless flights of stairs they trudged, every room filled with illusions that had saved Maurice money. Artwork painted in manure, bannisters fashioned from cardboard tubes, chocolate fireguards – there was no corner he wouldn't cut. It was mind-boggling for Masher. *My dad is the smartest bloke in town!* he thought. No one else would have the imagination to do this.

As Maurice led him through the garage, he gave Masher a final grin.

'Remember the rats I told you about? The sea of them that were living here before?'

'Yeah,' Masher answered, looking around nervously in case one might be about to run over his foot.

'Well, I decided not to evict them. Didn't seem fair, especially as I'm a big-hearted man. So I put them to work instead.'

'What do you mean?'

'You see, putting in a boiler for a house this big would cost me a fortune, so I did some maths and realised I could do it much more cheaply . . .'

With a flourish, Maurice bowed and pulled open a secret trap door.

The sight that greeted Masher almost blew the top of his head off. There, in a subterranean lair, were hundreds and hundreds of plastic hamster wheels, all spinning madly thanks to a legion of rats. From each wheel ran a wire, which led, in turn, to a rickety old generator.

'Every time a wheel spins, it creates power. Enough to power the house, well, until the rats snuff it anyway.'

'When will that be?' Masher asked.

'Long after the contracts have been signed.'

'But it'll stink won't it? Once they've died. I mean, they'll be rotting down there. It'll be a nightmare for the owners.'

Maurice smiled at his son, and punched him affectionately on the arm.

'Ah, my boy. You've a lot to learn. Estate agents like us? We're in the dream business. We show people their dream houses, they fall in love with the dream and buy the house. It's only idiots who don't know that all dreams have to end. It's only idiots who don't realise that some dreams turn into nightmares. That's not my fault, it's just a fact of life.'

Masher looked into his dad's face. This was no wind-up or mickey-take. His dad was telling the truth. This was how life worked and Masher felt lucky his dad was such a brilliant teacher.

'Come on, son.' Maurice beamed. 'It's time I got you home. I've another surprise waiting for you.'

'Is it them boots? The one with the steel toecaps and pop-out spikes?' Masher had been eying them for months.

'Better than that, son. I've been cooking up a plan. Step one in Storey Street domination. We're starting with that dump next door, but this time next year the whole street will be ours, all ours!'

And with the kind of laugh reserved for a Hollywood villain, Maurice led his son back to their car.

5. A Revolting Revolt

Masher and Maurice purred onto Storey Street in their luxury motor, only to hit a traffic jam, not consisting of cars or bikes, but children.

Kids of all ages, the kids who lived in the posh semis as well as the terraced houses, were all out on the street, each of them clutching an official-looking letter, and each of them wearing the angriest expression.

'Ha!' laughed Maurice. 'Word's out, it seems. Look at them, pathetic little worms.'

Masher's forehead creased like a badly-ironed shirt. 'Word about what, Dad?' he asked.

The car came to a stop as the crowd surrounded Masher's car door.

'I'll let them tell you, son. A good estate agent has to think on his feet sometimes. And as you're a chip off the old block, you'll put this rabble in their place quick-smart.' He unclipped his seatbelt, before leaning into his son with one more bit of advice. 'Look them in the eye, son . . . and remember, you're a Milner.' And he pushed past the kids into the house, growling at the them as he went.

Masher paused momentarily in his seat. Not out of fear. Masher didn't do fear. This was more confusion. Dad didn't normally talk in riddles, and as a result, Masher hadn't a clue what he was walking into. Still, he had to remember what Dad said. He was a Milner, and a Mashing one at that. So, without further hesitation, he threw open his door, taking out seven of the baying mob in the process.

'What's up with you lot?' he boomed.

He was met with a chorus of boos and hisses. Kids that normally wouldn't dare look at him were giving him the evil eye. Whatever Dad had done, it had got right under their skin.

'As if you didn't know!' shouted Danny Christmas, though he shouted it from behind a dozen other children. 'Show him the letter. That'll jog his memory.'

Two dozen sheets of A4 were shoved under Masher's nose. Masher responded by ripping up six of them, and blowing his nose on three, before finally reading one.

He read it hungrily too, hoping all the answers would lie in the letter in front of him.

It read:

Dear Resident of Storey Street,

It has come to our attention that an area of your road has lately fallen into a dilapidated and unruly state.

Worse than this, we are told it has become a place of vandalism, where unruly youths meet to make mischief and misery for others.

Thankfully, your neighbours, the upstanding and community-minded Milner family, have agreed to help us with this issue, since the space in question sits next to their home.

Despite us searching for at least three lunchtimes, we, the council, have not been able to identify to whom this land (referred to by the rabble who currently use it as 'The House That Was Stolen') belongs, and so the Milner family has, at great expense, offered to buy it from us, and will extend their current family home across it.

The council has decided that the true owners of this 'stolen' house have one month from today to reclaim their property. If they do not do so, and if the site remains empty, apart from a settee, TV and lamp, then we will be delighted to accept the Milners' kind and generous offer.

Yours Blah-de-blah-blah-blah,

Stanley Albertson
Mayor and Master Butcher,
(Albertson and Son and Son, purveyors of
award-winning sausages since pigs were invented)

Masher felt a grin widen across his face. He'd had no idea his dad had been plotting this, but buying The House That Was Stolen was a stroke of genius. By doing so, they'd drive out the idiots that used it at the moment AND establish themselves as the most powerful residents of Storey Street. If Masher knew his dad, he wouldn't stop there. Bit by bit, house by house, the Milners would take over. If his dad wanted to make every house on the street theirs and turn it all into one Milner Mega-Mansion, that was exactly what would happen. No one could get in their way.

'I don't know what you lot are getting so upset about. I mean, look at this place – it's a dump. There're probably rats living in that settee, and as for the TV and lamp? They don't even have plugs, you nuggets!'

'Who cares if the settee's lumpy, or the TV isn't digital?' Elliot yelled, to the nods of Danny Christmas and the others. 'It's our space. Always has been and always will be. I learned how to play football here and so did my dad.'

'I learned to ride my bike here,' shouted another small voice.

'I read my first book on that settee,' yelled another.

'And I use the back corner as a loo when my mum and dad are out and I can't get in the house!' called Timmy Bentone from Number 37, only to be met with a look of disgust from everyone.

'And that sums up why we're buying it,' said Masher. 'To stop divots like you abusing it. So if I were you, I'd back off and stay out of my way. Otherwise you'll feel my wrath.'

And with the strut of a lazy cat who's won a lifetime supply of mousetraps, Masher strode home, to worship at the feet of his genius father.

6. Don't Panic . . .

. . . Which is easy for me to say. After all, I'm just the wally who writes these stories down. For the kids of Storey Street, the news of the proposed Milner Mansion had gone down like a sausage roll at a vegetarian banquet.

The second Masher's front door closed, an emergency meeting was called at The House That Was Stolen.

'Listen!' yelled Danny Christmas, who wasn't much of a shouter. 'Settle down, will you?'

No one listened, even after the fifth attempt. The crowd was way too boisterous. Only when Elliot Tipps stood on top of the TV and SCREAMED did thirty-three mouths close and look his way. Bodies piled onto the settee, so many fitting on its groaning body that they set a new world record without even knowing it.

'We all know why we're here,' Danny began nervously. 'To address the greatest threat ever posed to us, the kids, the most important people on Storey Street.'

There was a chorus of agreement and Danny continued:

'This is our house. It's always been ours, just like it belonged to our parents before us.'

More cheers, louder this time.

'Now I don't know about you, but I'm not going to just sit here and let those meathead Milners take it from us. Not without a fight.'

'No way,' yelled a girl called Floss, who was the greatest eleven-year-old film director ever. 'I'm premiering my new movie here next month and I WON'T hold it anywhere else, not even Hollywood!'

'Plus we've got the Seacross Domino Championships the week after that!' yelled Laszlo Di Bosco.

'And the Eating Donuts Without Licking Your Lips Final the Sunday after!' yelled a chubby child called Charlie.

This was music to Danny's ears. 'And we can't cancel any of these things, can we?'

'No way!' the crowd roared back, louder than a pride of livid lions.

'We need a plan. A brilliant plan, a cunning plan. A plan more watertight than a mermaid's bathtub. So what are we going to do?'

The roaring stopped. Silence reigned, except for the hammering of Danny's jackhammer heart.

Together, they sat for a good minute, until Timmy Bentone jumped to his feet, eyes full of urgency.

'What?' asked Danny. 'What's your idea?'

'I need a wee!' Timmy yelled and legged it home, not daring to use the outdoor facilities any more.

The crowd sighed and settled back into further silence.

'Could we start a petition?' asked Jake Biggs.

'No point,' said Danny. 'My dad reckons Maurice Milner has already bribed the council.'

'Why don't we secretly knock down the Milners' current house?' suggested Jack Boo excitedly. 'If we do that, then they won't be able to afford to build the new one.'

'How are we going to do that?' scoffed Elliot Tipps. 'How do you secretly knock down a house?'

'Oh, you know, a few bricks at a time . . .'

'And you don't think they'd notice?' said Elliot. 'It might be a bit draughty when half their living room wall has "mysteriously" disappeared!'

A lot of the other kids laughed riotously. Elliot was one of those annoying, popular kids who could read out a chip shop menu and folk would laugh, just to be his friend.

'Well, I don't see *you* coming up with anything!' said Jack, blushing.

'Yeah,' agreed Danny, who knew how rubbish it was to be laughed at. 'Let's hear your plan, Elliot!'

Elliot looked momentarily panicked, before standing straight and saying, 'Simple, isn't it? We club together and buy the

Milners a new house. A house that isn't even on Storey Street.'

Elliot looked smug. So smug you'd think he'd just invented a vacuum cleaner that not only tidies your room but does your homework as well.

The others, awestruck, rapidly emptied their pockets and counted up the spoils.

'£13.67, a conker and a broken pencil sharpener,' Danny said, deadpan, as he tapped at his phone. 'According to the Internet, that'll buy us a one-bedroomed cardboard box under the motorway bridge.'

Groans all around.

'At least it's got good transport links,' Elliot blushed.

'This is getting us nowhere,' said Danny. 'We've got thirty days to find the owners of The House That Was Stolen. And thirty days to make sure they don't sell it to the Milners. We need to be methodical. We'll split into three teams. Team A will be responsible for Internet research. Their job is to plough through every page on the web that relates to Storey Street. There's got to be something on there that throws up a clue about who owns this place. Or something that helps us claim it legally as ours!'

A wave of nodding heads rippled round the crowd, followed by a smattering of volunteers.

'What about Team B?' asked Jake.

'Team B will be foot soldiers. They are going to knock on every single door in Seacross and show them a picture of the house, and they're not going to stop until it jogs someone's memory. There are some really old people living in this place. Someone must remember something.'

More volunteers volunteered, as volunteers do.

'And Team C?'

'Team C will be our warriors. There's a possibility that despite the Googling and door-knocking, we might not dig anything up. So we're going to set up a protest. We're going to sit here with banners twenty-four hours a day and light a fire in a bin, and every time a builder or an architect or a Milner tries to set foot on our property, we're going to make life very unpleasant for them.'

This was met with the biggest roar of them all, a rallying call of a group of children hell-bent on preserving what was rightfully theirs.

Well, all except for Jack Boo, who'd seen a couple of flaws in Danny's plan.

'The protest is a great idea, but I can't do it twenty-four hours a day. My mum says I have to be in half an hour before sunset, and only if my homework's done. And as for the fire in the bin? Well, this is awkward, but . . . I'm not allowed to play with matches.'

The children of Storey Street looked at Jack agog. He was a good kid, with a big heart, but what on earth was he talking about?

'Then we'll just have to find a way of fooling your mum Jack, won't we?' said Danny, as sympathetically as he could. 'Adopt Milner-esque tactics.'

'What do you mean?' asked Jack.

'We lie and we cheat and we do whatever it takes, by any means necessary, to make our mission a success. Prepare yourself, people, because tomorrow, we FIGHT!'

And with that last rallying call, the children of Storey Street dispersed for tea.

Tomorrow was day one in their war against the Milners.

But when it arrived, it wouldn't be the day they were expecting.

7. Strangers in the Night

Masher woke up hungry, but not for breakfast. There was no cereal, toast or sausage sandwich on his menu, only pain and misery, served cold.

Yesterday should have been epic for Masher, as his dad's dastardly plan went public. But by the end of it, it had felt frustrating and boring. By teatime he'd barely Mashed a single person all day, which left him feeling restless. Even thirty minutes on his punchbag couldn't sate his appetite, so instead he'd gone hunting up and down the length of Storey Street, only to find empty streets. Confused, he'd peered through windows to see some kids frantically scouring their computer screens and making notes, while others grouped together in living rooms, paintbrushes in hand.

He'd had no idea what they were up to, and wouldn't have cared, had it not left him with no Mashing options whatsoever.

Masher didn't even have his own gaggle of moronic counterparts to pass time with. He used to, in the shape of classmates Saliva Shreeve and Bunions Bootle, but Dad had felt them too wet, too polite for Masher's company, and had banned his son from playing with them.

Which left Masher all on his lonesome. Eventually he'd admitted defeat and gone home to his own computer, where he'd searched for things he could buy and hit.

As a result, today Masher felt like a bubbling pot of chilli, all spicy and volatile, and he pitied the poor kid who got in his way first.

Who would it be? He was a bit bored of pulverising Danny Christmas – I mean, there was no challenge in mashing such a massive wimp, but since Danny lived so close, it was always Masher's default option.

As he approached his bedroom window, Masher had a brainwave. He would let fate decide. He'd heard about people who lived their lives on the roll of a dice, letting chance decide everything for them. The thought excited him. That's what he'd do. Today he would Mash the first kid he saw, and only that kid, regardless of how old or tough they were.

Grabbing the curtains in his granite paws, Masher took a

deep breath and ripped them open, only to see not one potential victim on the street outside, but thirty-four of them. Now, Masher was a bully who liked a challenge, but even he couldn't manage to terrorise an army of kids in one day. It was possible to spread yourself too thin in life. As Masher began the arduous process of choosing just one, he saw that all the kids were carrying boards with writing on. Angry boards. And on some of them he could see his family's name.

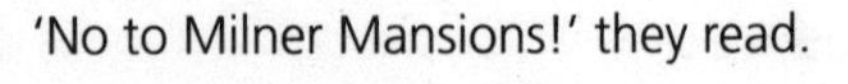

'No to Milner Mansions!' they read.

'Save our Street!'

'You'll Never Heist our House!'

'Down with This Sort of Thing!'

Masher's brain kicked into gear. What on earth was going on? They weren't protesting, were they? Those idiotic little chumps didn't seriously think they could go up against Masher's dad and win, surely?

Well, the answers were yes, they did think they could defeat Maurice Milner, and yes, they were protesting.

Or at least they'd planned to, except when they arrived at Masher's house they were faced with a sight that none of them could possibly have ever expected. And one that Masher couldn't even see from his window.

Not that he was standing at it any more. He was racing down the stairs, shouting aloud . . .

'Dad! Grandma! Quick! Come and see what those idiots are trying to do outside. It's HILARIOUS!'

The antique kitchen door, encrusted with highly expensive and tasteless bling, flew open and the Milner clan headed outside, to be met with a sight that twisted both their brains and their stomachs.

Somehow, someone, overnight, had managed to steal The House That Was Stolen.

Where there had once been a concrete gap, complete with its TV, lamp and settee, there was now an old-fashioned, but highly-polished metal caravan. So shiny and buffed was it that the protestors and the Milners could see their gaping expressions reflected back at them.

JESSOP

'Where did that come from?' gasped Danny, who didn't know whether to be relieved or anxious about who might live inside. I mean, he hated Masher, but what if these new people were even worse?

'How did they even park it there?' asked Jack Boo, which was an excellent question, as you couldn't have squeezed a credit card between the caravan and the wall at one side and the high wooden gate on the other.

Maurice Milner was livid. He needed the land ownerless and empty. Within seconds he was on his phone, calling Mayor Stanley Albertson directly, and shouting words so obscene they would make your dad blush. To be honest, they were so rude even I don't know what they mean. And I know a few rude words, believe me.

While Maurice ranted and raved, Masher and the other kids took in the sight in front of them.

Masher was shaking his head in confusion. His dad's plan was so incredible, he couldn't believe anyone or anything could get in the way of it. He almost pitied the fools who dared to take him on.

The other kids were just as bemused. They'd thought only the Milners wanted to steal their land, but now it seemed there was another enemy to consider.

What if these newcomers were even more conniving?

As one, they looked around for clues. It was surprising enough to see a caravan slap-bang in the middle of their patch, but there were other things to take in, too.

Like a front lawn, for starters, which sat in front of the caravan, its grass so lush it looked as if it'd been laid a hundred years ago. There were flowerpots and beds around the edges, with roses in full bloom. On a birdfeeder sat a collection of robins, larks and even a woodpecker, all feasting away merrily.

'How did they do this?' asked Masher, who was a boiling mess of anger and confusion.

'I've no idea,' said Maurice, off the phone now and scowling around him. 'But they're going to pay, believe me.'

Eyes flicked everywhere, taking in other details: the telephone wire that ran from the van to a pylon across the street; the white picket fence that had been erected at the very front, complete with mailbox and a word stencilled carefully into the side of it.

'Jessop', it read, simply.

'Jessop?' Masher roared. 'JESSOP! They must be Jessops if they think they're going to get away with this.'

A couple of the kids dared to giggle in the bully's direction, but soon stopped when he picked them up by their ears and hurled them into the gutter.

'Here,' yelled Elliot Tipps, who was hoping against hope that he'd be allowed to play footie on the beautiful lawn. 'There's a cage in the corner there, too.'

He was right, there was, and how everyone had missed it at first was baffling. It was a large cage, too big for a dog, even a Great Dane or St Bernard. Its sides were made from solid oak panels, whereas the front looked more like the sort of cage you saw at a zoo, the sort that housed animals with sharp teeth and a penchant for eating children who wandered too close.

'What in the name of Satan's bottom is in there?' whimpered Kay Catt, a member of the Scaredy Catt family, who, having bravely come outside, was now wishing she hadn't.

'I'm going to find out,' said Elliot. 'Can't be anything dangerous. Not on a street like this.' And he walked through the gate, towards the cage.

'What can you see?' asked Danny.

'Nothing yet. It's pretty dark in there. It's probably empty.'

But as Elliot edged closer, he was suddenly met by a roar so loud that it blew him clean off his feet and all the way across the garden. (Don't worry, he landed on his football, which cushioned the blow.)

With that, the crowd went into hysterics. Kids dashed about wildly, banging into each other and getting nowhere. Maurice Milner dropped his phone in shock and saw it trodden underfoot. Even Masher had an expression of undiluted fear on his face.

Then, just as the children ran to call the police, the army and probably The Avengers (if anyone had their mobile number), a new noise erupted from the caravan, this time from a tannoy, which they now saw was hooked to the top of it.

'Ladies and gentlemen, be not afraid. Twinkles means you no harm . . . and besides, you don't want to run away now . . . the show is about to begin . . .'

Panic eased a jot, the children overcome by curiosity and downright nosiness, as the front door flew open and out flowed a cloud of dry ice, followed by a HUGE shadow that seemed to fill every centimetre of the skyline . . .

8.

At Home with the Jessops

'Laydeeez and gentlemen, boys and girls, neighbours, friends,' boomed the voice, as its body loomed out of the fog. 'Please don't be afraid. We aren't here to scare you. We're here to please, to illuminate . . . and most importantly, to entertain!'

The crowd gasped as the figure became fully visible. A man mountain he was, well over two metres tall, with a torso so chiselled it looked as if he'd been carved from the slopes of Everest. Over his muscled torso struggled a red suit jacket with tails, although it barely contained his power. On his legs were a pair of tight, black leggings, hugging his thighs and calves.

The man's face was equally rugged, with cheekbones that seemed to have been constructed in a maths lesson with a protractor and set square. He was handsome, smooth and debonair, and proved it by intermittently twirling his moustache with fingers thicker than Danny Christmas's arms. He wasn't

cocky, though, just confident, with eyes that danced with warmth.

'My name is Jeremiah Jessop: strongman, escapologist, ringmaster.'

As if to prove his strength he strode forward and effortlessly plucked Elliot Tipps, Jack Boo and Danny Christmas from the ground. With a flick of his wrists, Danny was catapulted onto Jeremiah's head, where he sat like a stunned pigeon at the top of Nelson's Column. Elliot and Jack were used like dumbbells as the ringmaster lifted them time and again. There were 'oooh's and 'aaah's and a smattering of confused applause as he returned the boys to the ground.

'But most importantly, I am husband and father to the most remarkable family in the world. Let me introduce you to my wife, Jacqueline Jessop: contortionist, acrobat, philatelist.'

Cue more 'oooh's and 'aaah's, plus a few 'eh's as the kids scratched their heads at the word philat … philatel … Oh, blimey, it's a hard word to type, never mind say. Why didn't he just say she collected stamps?!

Anyway, regardless, from the doorway sprung a woman in a violet leotard, her body spinning and whipping around as she performed a triple back somersault with six and a half twists.

It was like watching a tornado pass over their heads.

With a flourish, the woman landed on her feet, only to be picked up and flung into the air again by her husband.

What was he doing? thought Danny. He'd thrown his wife so high and with such force she'd be needing a spacesuit, or a parachute at the very least. But as the woman began to plummet, destined for life as a splat on the pavement, she twisted, grabbing onto a telephone wire that ran across the street. With a shimmy and a loop-the-loop the woman landed, cat-like, on the line and proceeded to dance her way along it, never once looking in danger of losing her balance. In fact, after half a minute she started to look distinctly bored and began bouncing on the wire as if it was a trampoline. With another flourish, she catapulted skywards, and leaning backwards, arranged herself into the shape of a wheel.

'HOW is she doing THAT??' shouted Danny.

'I have no idea,' answered Elliot. 'But if she lands on the floor like that she'll have more than a puncture to deal with.'

Jacqueline Jessop didn't land on the floor. Of course she didn't. Instead she came to rest on the wire and proceeded to roll, forwards and backwards, at varying speeds, until she paused over her front garden. Then, with a graceful swan dive, she allowed herself to fall, into the beefcake arms of her adoring husband.

The crowd went mental. Even the kids momentarily forgot that their precious turf had been invaded. But the Jessops weren't finished yet. Instead, Jeremiah silenced the crowd with a finger to his lips.

'And finally, let me introduce you to our pride, our joy, and the right and future heirs to the family legacy: our children, Jemima and John-boy Jessop!'

Attention flew back to the caravan door, where a small, athletic figure zoomed into view, which at first sight seemed to have two heads, and a wheel instead of legs.

'What's going on? What sort of monster is this? Oh my lord, whatever it is, it's probably going to eat us!' squealed Kay (Scaredy) Catt.

But this was no monster. What it was, was two people, just as Jeremiah had said. A young girl of about ten years old riding a unicycle, with a wee boy (I mean that he was small, not that he was using the toilet) perched on her shoulders. Even more remarkable was that the boy couldn't have been more than four years old. Regardless, there John-boy sat, beaming widely as his sister pedalled furiously around the crowd at the sort of speed a moped could only dream of. Round and round they tore, faster and faster, until John-boy took the danger to new levels by juggling. With knives!

By this point Masher felt as if his head was going to fall off. Where had these freaks come from? And more importantly, how long were they staying? He looked to his dad, who was thumping a text into a shattered-looking mobile phone.

'Bah! I bet those knives aren't even REAL!' he yelled.

'Who cares?' came the answer, and they were right. Who did care? It was the most amazing thing anyone on Storey Street had ever seen. And they had seen some things, believe me . . . Anyway, you should already know that. Have you not read the other books in the series? Honestly, really, tut tut . . .

For Danny Christmas, it was a life-changing moment. Everyone experiences them at one point. For some, it's the moment they go to a football match for the first time; for others, their first skydive over hostile enemy territory (no? Just me?), but for Danny, it was the first time he ever laid eyes on Jemima Jessop.

It could be argued that her little brother was the more talented – after all, he was the four-year-old, juggling knives on the shoulders of his sister – but there was something about JJ (as Danny was already calling her in his head) that made his heart sing and his head throb. All right, he might have been a little bit in lurve with her already, but there was more than that, something he couldn't put his finger on.

She was just so . . . confident. And fearless. As she pedalled that wheel around, faster and faster without ever falling off, she managed to give the crowd eye contact and a smile.

Bringing the show to a thrilling end, Jemima rode the unicycle up a bridge made of her mother's body, until she reached the arms of her adoring father.

Then, without hesitation or difficulty, Jeremiah lifted his son, daughter, unicycle and wife high above his head, before a confetti cannon exploded behind them, showering everyone, and I mean everyone, in multi-coloured ticker tape.

What followed was a roar never before heard in the northern hemisphere, as the crowd forgot their concerns and welcomed the Jessops.

It was a fairytale happy ending, or at least it was until it was punctured by a mud pie hurled in the Jessops's direction. A mud pie that landed, splat and flush, on Jemima's face.

There was a gasp from the crowd. No one had expected this encore and they turned as one to stare at the person who'd thrown it.

And who did the dirty hands belong to?

Yep, you guessed it.

Our good friend, Masher Milner.

9.

They Come in Peace . . . or Maybe Pieces

Time stood still. Well, it didn't, obviously, because time waits for no man, or woman or child or dog for that matter, but you're missing the point. What I mean is, when Masher threw that mud pie, everyone was shocked, which made it feel like time stood still.

OK? Clear? Good.

It wasn't much of a welcome, that was for sure, especially after the feast the Jessops had just served up.

'Oi! Maurice Milner,' yelled George Biggs, who, as a former wrestler, was not a man to be trifled with. 'You need to keep that boy of yours on a lead if that's the way he treats people.'

There was a chorus of agreement from the others, who knew only too well what Masher was capable of. Not that Masher cared, so he replied with a sweary word.

'And with a potty mouth like that, he should have a muzzle too,' George said.

With that, Storey Street started to resemble a war zone, except the bullets were verbal instead of literal.

Maurice Milner didn't take kindly to his son being insulted, and started to square up to George. In return, George pulled himself to his full, gargantuan height and prepared to body slam Maurice into submission.

They would have gone at it too, had the even more imposing figure of Jeremiah Jessop not gently squeezed between them.

'Gentlemen, gentlemen,' he cooed, in a tone so soft it belied his might. 'Please, there is no need for this aggression. Not on my family's behalf. Perhaps we should've announced our arrival more gently, to lessen the tension. Or perhaps, simply, our performance wasn't up to scratch. I'm not entirely happy with the way I hoisted the children skywards at the end there. Maybe we deserve such interesting and creative criticism. Either way, be angry with us, not each other.'

George Biggs took a step backwards. He was a good man, a decent man, not prone to seeking out confrontation for fun. He still didn't like the way Masher had acted, not one little bit, but there was such calmness about Jeremiah that he couldn't help but be infected by it.

Maurice Milner, however, was so angry he'd barely listened

to a word Jeremiah had said, apart from the bits that suited him, which he lobbed straight back in the ringmaster's face.

'I'm not interested in gentle introductions, not from the likes of you. You could put a full-colour advert in the Seacross Gazette and I still wouldn't be impressed.' This was actually a bit of a lie. Maurice was constantly advertising his estate agency in the Seacross Gazette, and took great delight in showing the ads to anyone who'd listen.

'Yeah, we don't want you here at all,' piped Masher. 'Who do you think you are? Pitching up with your tin can caravan and your bendy wife and your weird kids? YOU. ARE. NOT. WELCOME. HERE.'

Now these words, my friends, are not kind words. They are not words anyone should utter, whether in truth or in jest. But although Masher was the only person to say them, there were other people in the crowd who weren't too happy about the Jessops's arrival either.

Despite the show they'd just witnessed, a number of the kids were muttering to each other, 'Hang on, what are these people doing on our patch?'

All right, they might not be as awful as Masher and his family, but they had still stolen their stolen house. What if they were as bad as the Milners?

Nervously, Danny Christmas stepped forward with Elliot, Jack and Floss, and spoke on behalf of them all.

'Excuse me, Mr Jessop. I'm not sure we'd put it like Masher, but you see, this space here where your caravan is, well, it's ours. It's where we hang out, play football, watch telly. It kind of belongs to us kids.'

Masher scoffed and pretended to throw up, but Danny wasn't put off.

'But with you arriving, where are we supposed to go?'

Jeremiah Jessop sighed, his eyes full of pain. 'Oh, my dear old thing.' He smiled sadly. 'I do understand, of course I do. We noticed as soon as we arrived that this was a sacred place, and the last thing we want to do is get in anyone's way, so we took the liberty of ... well, why doesn't Jemima show you?'

Obediently, Jemima sprang into action, and with a sprightly 'HELLO!' to the kids she opened the gate to the side of the caravan and shepherded the crowd through.

Jaws fell open, but fortunately nobody's flies, although you'd have been forgiven for weeing yourself in excitement when you saw what the Jessops had prepared behind their caravan. First, there was more grass, cut short and marked into a neat five-a-side footie pitch. Elliot Tipps ran and dived head first to embrace it. Then there was a settee – not a tatty three-seater like the old one, but an L-shaped, bus-sized, comfort-fest of a settee, big enough to seat a small army. Beside it stood a number of lamps, perfectly positioned for reading under the cover of darkness, and to top it off, a 44-inch plasma screen smart TV with high-speed, fibre-optic Wi-Fi built in. The Jessops had even constructed a canopy over the settee and telly so the kids could still relax there if it was raining.

'We hope you like it.' Jemima smiled. 'We'd have liked to do more, but time was tight.'

Well, it's fair to say that in that moment, the children of Storey Street welcomed the Jessops wholeheartedly. One kid even started adoption proceedings in the hope of a new and better life.

'This is amazing!' said Danny to himself.

'This is . . . terrible,' mouthed Masher to his dad. How had this happened? How had a plan so good gone so wrong so quickly? His dad, for once, was speechless.

'They might be different, this family,' shouted Elliot Tipps, as he rolled on the grass like a soppy Labrador, 'but that doesn't mean we should kick 'em out. Let's give 'em a chance, I say!'

Elliot wasn't the only one feeling this. Danny Christmas wanted to worship at the Jessops's altar, as by occupying the land they threw a whole toolbox into the Milners' works, never mind a spanner.

It was a spanner that Masher wanted to use, preferably on the Jessops's caravan.

'We've enough freaks living on this street, without adding to them,' he growled at Elliot and Danny. 'Mind you, Christmas, your conk is so red they'd probably give you a job as their freak show clown.' Masher found his own comic intellect staggering, and looked to his dad for a pat of appreciation. Maurice, however, hadn't heard his son's comment. His brain was too fixated on the problems that the Jessops had created.

'Regardless of what anyone else thinks, you can't stay here any longer!' Masher shouted. 'This space is spoken for.'

'Yes, we've heard about the plans for your new house,' replied Jemima, smiling sweetly at him.

Masher was confused.

'You've heard? How?'

'When you live on the road you hear a lot of things on the breeze. It all sounds phenomenally exciting. I hear the council have a month to find the rightful owners before the bricklayers arrive.'

'I don't care what you've heard. You'll be gone by tonight if you've any sense.'

The words that fell out of Masher Milner's mouth were a threat. He knew it, Jemima knew it, even you and I, dear reader, know it. But Jemima didn't respond with threats of her own, and nor did her dad, who addressed Milner Senior.

'My dear Mr Milner, or can I call you Maurice, in the spirit of neighbourliness? We've no interest in causing you grief. Of course not. That isn't the Jessop way, especially when the welcome has been so wonderfully overwhelming.' He beamed at the crowd, who beamed right back. 'My only hope is that, as time goes on, you'll learn to love us. You don't need to spend money laying more bricks. Our house is your house too, and our door is always open. You can walk through it whenever you wish.'

And with that, Jeremiah and his remarkable family started to mingle with the crowd, shaking hands and making friends.

The Milners were incandescent (bright-bright-bright-bright red) with rage. What was it Jeremiah had actually said? The man talked in riddles. Riddles that had hypnotised the rest of the crowd. Well, it wasn't going to work on them.

As Maurice fought to find the right response, Masher took the matter into his own hands. He reckoned he knew how to turn the other families against the Jessops immediately. Through fear.

So as the kids all patted themselves on the back, Masher strode confidently back through the gate onto the perfect front lawn and towards the cage in the corner.

'Where's he off to?' Danny said to Elliott. He knew Masher well enough to know he was up to no good. Dragging as many adults and kids with him as possible, he followed after the bully.

They found Masher beside the mysterious cage, wrestling

with the padlock on its door. Masher knew that if he could prove that whatever was in this cage was not suitable for life on a quiet residential street, the Jessops would be hounded away in minutes.

Just as the padlock started to twist in his hands, Masher was confronted with a sight that took a bite from his soul. Out of the darkness loomed two piercing green eyes, glistening like the most priceless of emeralds. If that wasn't terrifying enough, there followed a row of jagged top teeth, then a bottom set too, creating a waterfall of saliva which dripped in Masher's direction.

The bully felt his knees buckle, his hands made useless by the tremors that shook through them. He wanted to back away but all he could do was listen, as a noise audible only to him reached into his ears.

I cannot repeat what was said to him; it wasn't really a word.

All I can say is that the noise rendered Masher powerless. At that moment he could not think, he could not speak; his very being was consumed by fear.

Only the sound of his father, repeatedly shouting in his direction, finally brought him back to his senses.

'Masher! Will you get away from that cage!'

The spell broken, Masher felt his legs begin to function again and he turned to face his dad.

'Hmmmphhhhbbhh,' he said, his mouth clearly not yet recovered.

'What on earth is WRONG with you?' Maurice said, looking his son up and down. 'And what is going on down there?'

Mashers eyes fell south, to his own trouser legs. His jeans, fortunately a dark, deep blue, were now looking a bit … well … soggy.

'Have you lost control of yourself?' Maurice whispered, appalled. 'In front of all these people?'

'Nnnngghhhhh,' replied Masher, not helping his cause.

'What have I told you about showing weakness?' his dad hissed. 'Now get in that house and clean yourself up, before anyone else notices.'

Masher watched the crowd as he stumbled home, hoping with all his might that no one had spotted what had happened.

But one person had. She might still have had mud pie in her eyes, but Jemima Jessop had seen Masher wet himself. She just chose not to tell anyone.

She was an astonishing person, that girl, as you will soon find out.

10.

The Milners Get Mean

It was all kicking off at Milner Mansions.

Father and son stomped around the house doing their best impressions of a couple of Rottweilers who'd been ruthlessly embarrassed by a family of cunning Chihuahuas.

Maurice had certainly lost his normal cool.

'It's your fault that folk out there are laughing at us,' he roared.

Eh? thought Masher. He didn't remember inviting that family of freakazoids to move in unannounced. He hadn't helped them lay the lawn or hammer in the picket fence. He knew better than to argue with his old man, though.

'I don't know what you were thinking, racing up to that cage. Haven't I told you before? Assess the situation before you plough in. "A failure to plan is a plan to failure!"'

Masher bit his lip in shame. Why hadn't he thought of that?

There was no way his dad would ever have done something so rash.

'And as for losing control of your bladder. Do we have to go online and buy you nappies now? Honestly!'

Grandma raised her eyes momentarily at the blissful thought of being able to bypass the toilet, but quickly returned to her knitting.

'I couldn't help it,' Masher gulped, 'You didn't see what I saw. It was evil, Dad. Whatever it is, it isn't human.'

'I don't care if you saw King bloomin' Kong. You'll be sucking your thumb again before we know it, and then how will I show my face in public, eh?'

'I'm sorry, Dad, honest I am.'

But Maurice wasn't interested in apologies; he'd already launched into full Crisis Management Mode. After selling crumbling houses as must-have mansions for the last two decades, he knew a thing or two about turning situations around. And he wasn't going to be foiled by a bunch of two-bit sideshow wannabes.

Masher watched as Maurice punched the mayor's number into his phone, saw his frustration rise as time and again he was kicked to voicemail.

'He's dumping my calls,' Maurice groaned.

'You could email him?' suggested Masher helpfully, but was met with a look so evil it could smash down walls.

Masher gazed at his feet and considered sewing his mouth up.

'I need a plan,' Masher's dad mumbled to himself. 'Come on, man, think! What do these people need to make 'em move on?'

Masher found himself trying to think too, pacing around in his dad's shadow, stroking his chin in the same perplexed way. Sequins! he thought. A huge trunk to bribe them with, so they could make new spangly outfits to wear as they travelled the rest of the world. But the more he thought about it, the less he wanted to say it out loud. Masher could've come up with the most watertight idea since someone held up a plastic tub and shouted, 'IT'S A BUCKET!!' and Maurice still would've sneered at him.

Maurice had an idea, though. 'Course he did. You didn't win Seacross Estate Agent of the Year fifteen years in a row by chance. Oh no. You won it by bribing people. So Maurice fetched a large black suitcase from under his bed.

'You're going on holiday?' Masher asked, confused.

'No, you numbnut.'

'Am I going on holiday?'

Dad didn't reply. Instead, he unzipped the case to reveal a HUGE amount of money. Mountains of the stuff, bundled neatly together and filling every centimetre of the case.

'There are only two languages these people understand,' Maurice said. 'One is violence, and . . . well, that Jeremiah is a bit bigger than me. The other is money. Money talks, son. And when it talks, people walk. And let's face facts, we want them to walk before the month is out. They might say they're staying, but one look at this lot . . . well, you'll see.' And he zipped up the case and walked to the door, Masher following like a lapdog.

'I don't think so. Let the master work alone.'

Masher waited as Dad strode purposefully towards the

Jessops's van. He watched as the door swung open and the hulking frame of Jeremiah shepherded Maurice inside.

The next five minutes were long and painful, filled with a lecture on knitting from Grandma, yet throughout those minutes, Masher's belief in his dad did not waver. He knew that once Dad did his thing, that caravan would quickly become a distant memory.

In fact, here came Dad now. Except he wasn't grinning like a victorious, corrupt gladiator, he was frowning. And he was still carrying the case, which looked full enough to buy a number of countries outright.

As Dad passed the cage in the Jessops's front garden, he was greeted by a blood-curdling roar, which made him scamper over the fence.

The front door slammed and Dad's suitcase whizzed past Masher's ears before bursting open, cascading the room with cash.

'They're bank robbers!' Maurice wailed. 'That's the only possible explanation.'

'Did you offer them the money?' asked Masher.

''Course I did. But he wouldn't have it. Said they had no need for it. He said they were richer than anyone else on the planet! So I asked him if he was an estate agent too. I mean, that has to be the answer, if he's so rich. Then he laughed again and told me I was the funniest person he'd ever met. Said we should all come round for dinner.'

'The cheek,' seethed Masher. 'Maybe he *is* an estate agent, from that new place in the precinct. Trying to get in on our turf, to send out a message.'

Maurice shook his head. 'The only thing sending out a message round here is that thing in the cage. Did you hear the noise it made at me as I went past?'

Masher nodded. It was probably the same noise it offered him, and by the look of Dad's trousers, it had had a similar effect.

But Maurice either didn't care about his little accident, or he simply hadn't noticed. For the first time since the Jessops's arrival, there was a sparkle in his eyes.

'Oh, they might think they're clever,' he purred. 'But you have to get up pretty darned early to get one over Maurice Milner. Give me a few days to hatch a campaign of revenge, and those Jessops will rue the day they ever stole our house!'

Yes! thought Masher. Dad was right. Tomorrow was another day, another chance to get rid of the nuisances next door. And he'd play his part. A BIG part.

And you know what? He was right.

11. Just the Two of Us

School. Torture for some, a place of heavenly delight for others.

For Danny Christmas, it was more often than not the former, thanks to Masher. But, as he left his house the next morning and stared at the Jessop caravan, he felt an unusual twinge of hope. As if something truly good was going to happen. He couldn't explain why, but there was something about that van and the oddballs living inside it that made him grin.

'Hello,' interrupted a voice, yanking Danny from his daydreams.

Jemima Jessop was standing beside him. How had she appeared from nowhere like that? Had she seen him staring at her van? Danny's nose glowed even redder than normal.

'It's Danny, isn't it?' she asked, voice chirpy.

'Yeah. How did you know that?' Danny replied.

'Name tag,' she said.

Now Danny was confused. Unless Mum had taken to stitching

name tags on his forehead instead of his school clothes, that didn't make sense.

'Eh?' he said. 'What?'

'Here.' She smiled, and with a deft flick of her hand, produced from Danny's left nostril a piece of fabric that she quickly unrolled. To his amazement, it read 'Danny Christmas'.

What? How? When? Danny was so bemused that he was tempted to ram his fingers up his nose and see what else was up there. His school jumper? His rucksack maybe? He didn't, of course. He covered his face with his hand. Was this Jemima's way of taking the mickey?

'What's the matter?' she asked, concern on her face. 'I haven't said something wrong, have I?'

'No it's just . . .' Danny mumbled from behind his hand.

'I've embarrassed you, haven't I? I'm SO sorry. I have a habit of saying the wrong thing when I first meet people. Pressure of moving around all the time, I guess. I feel like I have to make friends quickly.'

She spoke as skilfully as she rode the unicycle.

'It's fine. I just, well, I'm a bit sensitive about this.' He pointed to his traffic light of a schnozz. 'Some people take the mickey out of me for it.'

'Ah,' she said. 'One person in particular, I'd imagine.'

Danny remembered what Masher had done to Jemima yesterday and blushed furiously again. It felt as if he'd thrown the mud pie himself.

'I'm sorry about Masher. I would say he's not normally like that, but, to be honest, he is. Worse, sometimes.'

'To you?'

Danny didn't know how to answer that. Masher was horrible to everyone, but on the especially bad days, it felt like the bully had been put on earth simply to torment him.

'What has he done?' Jemima continued.

'Oh, you know, just the usual. Tied me to my desk with fairy lights, made me floss my teeth with tinsel, stuck a couple of baubles up my nose.'

Jemima looked confused.

'Because of my surname. Christmas?'

'Ah, I get it. Sort of. The play on words bit, I mean, not why it's funny.'

'Wait till you hear what my dad does, then you'll laugh. Father bloomin' Christmas.'

Well, I might be laughing dear reader (not at Danny, merely at the ridiculousness of his dad's name – chuckle), but Jemima retained the straightest of faces, while thinking long and hard.

'Hhhm,' she said eventually. 'He must be really unhappy.'

'Who? My dad? Why? He loves his job.'

'No, not your dad. Masher.'

It was Danny's turn to fall silent. Masher? Unhappy? Boy oh boy, was she barking up the wrong tree.

'Are you kidding me? Masher lives to bully. He didn't get that nickname by accident.'

He expected Jemima to come back with a counterargument, but she didn't bother. She just smiled and shrugged, leaving Danny to ponder what Masher possibly had to be unhappy about. Were his fists not hard enough? Boots not steely enough? Danny couldn't work it out, and refused to believe it. So he changed the subject.

'I can't believe you arrived overnight and still managed to make our space look so amazing. It looks like you've been there for years.'

'Just practice.' Jemima shrugged. 'When you've done it as often as us, you get the hang of it.'

'Anything that upsets Masher is all right by me. The longer you stay, the better.'

'Ach, that's enough about him,' Jemima said. 'We should be getting to school, shouldn't we?'

'You're coming to our school?'

'Duh, yeah . . . Mum and Dad might be good at circus stuff, but they're rubbish at fractions. Come on, I'll just grab my bag.'

She spun off towards the caravan, Danny trailing excitedly behind her.

'Come in a sec,' she shouted as she leaped gracefully through the door.

It's fair to say that Danny's expectations of inside the van were already pretty high, but as his eyes acclimatised to the darkness, his jaw dropped to the floor. It was massive. So big, it made the Tardis look like a box room in a bungalow.

On every centimetre of the surfaces in the lounge were framed photographs – some modern, some ancient, each with one thing in common: they contained images of incredible circus folk doing the most remarkable things. There were trapeze

artists, contortionists and animal tamers, photos of men with their heads in lions' mouths, photos of lions with their heads in men's mouths. I kid you not, look!

'Are these people all your family?' Danny asked.

'They are. I come from a long line of Jessops.'

Danny wasn't sure he ever wanted to leave that room. In fact, he wanted to be a Jessop more than he'd ever wanted anything in his life. They were all so talented, whereas he struggled to tie his own laces in a double knot without losing his balance.

'Wow, it must be amazing, being in your family.'

'Sometimes,' said Jemima. 'Performing's what we do, and I love it, but it'd be nice to do it in the same place for a while.'

'Well, that place is here!' Danny said.

'Hopefully, but it's hard to settle when some people don't like the fact that we're . . . different.'

'Different's not the right word for you, no chance. Unique. That's the one!'

'You're very kind, Danny Christmas. Kinder than most.'

'What, you mean Masher?'

Jemima smiled. 'No, not him, not really. He's just unhappy, remember?'

Danny frowned. 'Why do you keep saying that? How can he

possibly be unhappy when he spends his life doing the one thing that he loves?'

Jemima's face gave nothing away, and neither did her mouth. Instead she smiled again, before picking up her bag and shouting in a SUPER-LOUD voice,

'I'M GOING NOW! SEE YOU AFTER SCHOOL!'

Danny had no idea how far away her parents were, but from the volume of Jemima's voice, it sounded as if they might have been in Australia.

As his ears stopped ringing, Danny heard Jacqueline respond in a distant tone: 'OK, darling, see you tonight.'

Danny followed Jemima out of the door. How big the van really was, he had no idea, but he knew one thing: Storey Street needed the Jessops. With them here, the Milners couldn't touch The House That Was Stolen. And with them here, The House That Was Stolen was pure and utter luxury!

It was simple. The Jessops HAD to stay.

12.

Queen Bee / Top Dog

Starting a new school is a terrifying thing. Worse than a trip to the dentist, worse than a trip to the doctor, worse even than having your hair washed by your dad instead of your mum. Why are dads always so rough?

Masher lurked at the school gates and watched as his new nemesis unicycled towards him, her idiotic sidekick Christmas running along next to her. He hoped she was bricking it, that she'd do something stupid that would reveal a chink in her (admittedly, so far impressive) armour. One he could mercilessly exploit.

If Jemima was nervous, she didn't show it. Not when she zoomed past him through the school gates, not when people stared at her unicycle, not even when she was made to stand at the front of their class by their teacher, Miss Maybury, to introduce herself.

'So that's all there is to know about me,' she said, after

telling them about the places in the world she and her family had performed. Some of the countries were so obscure that Miss Maybury was furiously flicking through an atlas to check Jemima wasn't telling porky pies.

It was enough to have Masher fuming. He was gripping his desk so hard that his fingers made dents in it. Who did Jemima think she was? Strutting around like she was the boss. There was only one boss round here and that was him!

Jemima hadn't bragged, though. She'd talked modestly, without ever being shy. How she managed it, I have no idea, but boy oh boy, she was good.

The rest of the class thought so too, and those who'd missed her family's first performance were desperate for a demonstration.

'I'm sure we could do it all again,' Jemima said as she answered questions all the way through first lesson. Strangely enough, Masher didn't ask any, despite wanting to know when her and her family were going to leave!

Playtime was no less busy. Kids from the other classes waded in, wanting to see the acrobat in action.

It turned out they were going to get what they wanted too, just not in the way they'd expected.

'Oi! Jessop!' bellowed a voice above the excited din. 'You think you're Queen Bee around here now, don't you?'

It was Masher, of course, whose internal thermometer had by now reached dangerous, radioactive levels.

Jemima looked around her, as if expecting to see someone in a winged yellow and black T-shirt, gathering honey in their arms.

'Well, let me tell you,' continued Masher. 'We don't do bees round here, 'cos all the wasps have eaten 'em. Except the wasps aren't wasps at all, they're Milners, like me.'

Danny had to bite his tongue. He'd watched a lot of natural history documentaries and he was pretty sure that wasps didn't eat bees. They preferred fallen fruit and nectar, though he didn't think this was the time to mention it.

'So if you think you're Top Dog,' said Masher, 'then I chal—'

'I thought you said I was Queen Bee?' said Jemima.

'Eh?'

'A second ago you said I was Queen Bee, only now I'm Top Dog, and to be honest, I'm a bit confused about who I am, where I am, and why you're so upset about it.'

Some of the kids in the crowd giggled. Masher tried to silence them with his finest death stare, but it had no effect. They were too entranced by Jemima.

'So which is it? Do I have wings and a sweet tooth or four legs and fleas?'

More laughter, and more bafflement from Masher. He wasn't used to people speaking to him like this. She wasn't fighting back, not physically anyway, but he didn't know what to say. What was the right answer?

Not knowing was weird. It made him feel small. He thought he could feel his school shirt getting bigger as the muscles on his arms shrank. What would his dad do?

'A race!' he blurted.

'Huh?' said Jemima. 'I'm a race now? A race of bees or dogs?

'No. A running race. Between you and me. Round the playground, over the monkey bars and through the long jump pit. Two laps. Winner takes all.'

That'd teach her not to hog the limelight.

Jemima looked around. 'You know, I really like it here. It's not as hot as Australia, or as hilly as Nepal, but it's cool. All the same, I don't need to be the "winner" of it, and besides, we live in a caravan. If I did win it all, where would I keep it?'

She was doing that thing again, bamboozling Masher with

her words. Danny wasn't sure he quite understood either. Besides, after seeing the inside of the caravan, he reckoned she could fit most of Seacross in there easily.

'Don't you want to be Top Dog?' Masher snarled.

'I don't even want to be Queen Bee,' Jemima sighed.

'Maybe you aren't as impressive as everyone thinks. Maybe you're just a bit of a chicken. A chicken with a chicken mum, a chicken dad, and a runt of a turkey for a brother.'

Eyes fell back to Jemima. Except Danny's, who by this point was desperate to put Masher straight on the flaws in his natural history knowledge. If Jemima, Jeremiah and Jacqueline were chickens, how could John-boy be a turkey? Unless he was adopted, and Danny was pretty sure chickens didn't adopt as a general rule . . .

'OK,' said Jemima, shrugging. 'I'll take you on.'

'Winner takes all,' said Masher.

'You said that already.'

'Yeah, but I haven't said this. If you lose, Jessop, then you and your family leave. Tonight. And you don't come back.'

The stakes had been raised higher than the Empire State building while having a shoulder ride on the London Eye.

There's no way she'll go for that, thought Danny. Would she? *Please, Jemima,* his mind whirred. *Don't agree. He'll find a way to race dirty. He always does.*

But Jemima wasn't listening. How could she when Danny was only thinking these things, not saying them?

'No problem,' she answered, still smiling. 'And if you lose?'

Masher racked his brain, which took a good couple of seconds, given its limited size and capacity.

'Everyone here can call me by my real name for the rest of the term.'

An exciting buzz ripped through the crowd. NEVER would Masher settle for that indignity. He would often give Chinese burns to nursery school pupils for not bowing at his feet and calling him 'Sir Masher of Milner'.

'Sounds more than fair,' said Jemima, as she began to limber up. 'Two laps. Playground, monkey bars, long jump pit. Tell me when you're ready.'

But Masher already was.

'ReadysteadyGO!' he yelled, pushing Jemima to the floor with the almightiest whack, before legging it towards the bars.

An 'oooooh' bounced off the school walls, followed by an 'ooooow' from Jemima, who lay on the ground, rubbing her left knee.

By now Masher was swinging like a gibbon with a crew cut across the apparatus, laughing like he'd already won.

All he had to do was cross the line first and that was it. Challenge over. Game over. And more importantly, this book would be over . . . and none of us want that, now do we . . . ?
DO WE?

13.

The Tortoise & The Jessop

Aesop's Fables are brilliant, aren't they? You know the stories I mean: they're always dead short and sometimes funny, plus they have a moral to them, a message to live by. Like never eat yellow snow.

'The Tortoise and the Hare' is my favourite, where the slowest animal in the wood beats the fastest. Anyway, this race was just like that, sort of, except at the start you would've put the contents of your moneybox on Jemima romping home to victory. All right, Masher was big and powerful, but Jemima was nimble and bendy. She could do things that seemed scientifically impossible. Put a Jessop up against a hare, or in this case a gorilla, and the Jessop should walk it.

But thirty seconds into the race, the Jessop wasn't even standing, never mind walking. Jemima was still on the floor, clutching her knee.

'Come on, Jemima,' said Danny, helping her to her feet. Up ahead Masher was celebrating his genius by kissing his biceps. In his head he'd already won. Big mistake.

Grimacing, Jemima put her weight on both feet and exhaled slowly, eyes fixed on her opponent. Then she did the strangest thing. Instead of following Masher, she turned in the other direction.

'What are you doing?' said Danny. 'You're facing the wrong way.'

But she wasn't. What Danny had forgotten was that Jemima was a Jessop, and Jessops never did things the normal way. Sometimes they turned the norm completely on its head. (Jemima's great-great-great-great-granddad was Australian.)

Without warning, Jemima threw herself backwards onto her hands, her legs propelling her skywards. Then, with a speed usually associated with a leopard who has just devoured a crate of energy bars, she built a tumbling momentum that had her eating up the ground.

Within seconds, Masher's lead had quartered, and by the time he reached the long-jump pit for the first time, it had halved. The first time he glanced over his shoulder, he tried not to look too concerned, though he definitely picked up the pace. The second time he looked, it was just in time to see Jemima stop tumbling and throw herself into the air, tackling the monkey bars with the grace of a gold-medal gymnast.

Masher was worried. He couldn't comprehend the speed at which she was travelling. But just as it seemed Jemima would reach her opponent in seconds, she landed heavily on her bad knee, the shock of impact shuddering her so hard it almost knocked her teeth out.

'Don't stop, Jemima. You've almost got him!' Danny yelled, but she couldn't go on. Not like this. Instead she leaped forwards and landed on her hands, before running on them instead.

How is she doing this? panicked Masher. Most ten year olds couldn't even write neatly, yet here she was using her mitts to sprint on. The race wasn't won, and that bothered him.

On the competitors tore, bodies blurring as they hit the second lap. Masher still had a chunky lead, but his lungs were constricting, his face the colour of a vicar who has just farted in a lift. Jemima's cheeks were red too, but that was mostly due to gravity rather than fatigue.

As they hit the monkey bars, Masher had a narrow lead, and spread his bulk across the apparatus to stop Jemima passing by. But this was no obstacle to the young Jessop, who swung herself on top of the bars and hand-standed across them, easing past Masher in the process.

There was a delighted roar from the crowd and a gasp of despair from her opponent. Masher had practically had a lap's head start against a lame opponent and still she'd clawed it back.

His potential punishment started to gnaw at his brain.

He HATED being called Quentin, so how he'd cope with everyone calling him that, especially if he couldn't retaliate, he had no idea.

More importantly, he knew that if he lost this race, his dad would find out too. Seacross was a small place;

news got around faster than headlice. He wasn't sure he could cope with the shame of letting Dad down.

So he gritted his teeth and pushed hard, his muscular frame managing to close the gap, but as he reached the long jump pit, disaster struck.

In his haste, Masher hadn't seen a rake lying on the sand, and in true comedy cliché – I mean, style – he stood on its head, which sent the handle smashing into his nose, and him to the floor in agony.

Up ahead, Jemima was unaware of the carnage, and was a matter of metres from glory. Just as her knee tickled the finishing line, she glimpsed behind her, and stopped.

To any normal person, this would be the ideal time to gloat, laugh and make rude hand gestures at the person who wanted you out of their life. But Jemima was a Jessop, and Jessops weren't made that way.

Instead of throwing herself over the line she sprinted in the opposite direction, towards Masher. Without worrying about getting herself covered in blood, she helped him to his feet, and carried him forwards.

'What are you doing?' he asked, mystified and muffled.

'Helping, you doofus,' she answered quietly.

Well, that answer just about had Masher's head exploding. He'd read the word 'help' in the dictionary, but had no idea how it worked in the real world. It certainly wasn't something he'd put into practice.

Confusion levels were just as high in the crowd. Heads were scratched, questions asked, one kid had even gone on Google to find out why Jemima would be so nice to a complete and utter wazzock.

On Jemima paced, with Masher seemingly weightless in her arms, until, finally, they collapsed together over the finishing line in a dead heat.

'You OK?' she asked him.

'I didn't ask you to help me,' he replied.

Not exactly 'thank you', but Masher was confused as well as exhausted and pained. Why had she come back for him when she could have won the race and subjected him to the worst fate imaginable? There was no way he'd have done the same for her. Even if there hadn't been so much at stake, he'd still have taken the victory. That's what Dad had drilled into him all of his life.

'I know you didn't,' Jemima said. 'But you were hurt. I couldn't just walk away, could I?'

This sentence stung his ears. Walk away? What, like he had?

He felt his face burn with an emotion he didn't understand, but I can tell you what it was, dear reader. It was guilt. Pure and simple.

But as he'd never dealt in the stuff, Masher defaulted back to aggression. He pulled himself to his feet and wiped the blood from his nose.

'Yeah, well, this doesn't change nothing. We still want you off our land. And we won't stop till you've gone. Don't forget that.'

'I doubt I'll be able to.' Jemima smiled as the bully stormed away.

Once Masher was well out of range, Danny ran to Jemima. 'What was that all about?'

'Oh, nothing. Come the end of the month we'll be best buds,

Masher and me.'

'Yeah, right. You'll be telling me next that even after the trick he just tried to pull, he's still just unhappy.'

Jemima's expression didn't change. The gentle smile didn't leave her lips, not even for a second.

'More than ever,' she said. 'But not for long. I'll see to that.' And she hobbled to class, ignoring the pain that raged in her leg.

The Hound of the Baskerwotsit

An ear-splitting howl ruptured the night, full of destruction and pain.

It pulled Jemima, startled, from her sleep.

In fact, the only people on Storey Street who didn't stir were the Pulse family and the temporary guests who lay within their undertakers' shop.

Everyone else woke with a shock, but, knowing they lived on a sleepy street in a crumbly seaside town and not in the middle of a jungle, thought it was just a dream and rolled over again.

Come the morning, though, the residents of Storey Street soon realised that something beastly really had gone on overnight.

It started with a scream that had curtains twitching, then a shout of 'SWEET LORD!!' that saw keys turning in locks.

Within minutes there were so many people standing outside

of their houses that it looked like a street party had broken out. But there was no bunting or streamers to be seen, and there were no joyous, smiling faces – just an endless wave of scowls and anger.

'Look at my fence!' someone yelled.

'Never mind your fence, it's eaten our rabbit hutch!' shouted another.

'I can't believe this. The bonnet of our car's been half-bitten off!'

These weren't the ramblings of a bunch of fools who'd spent the night sniffing Pritt Stick. It was true: nearly every house on the road had been the victim of an attack. Flowers, hedges, fences, walls – there was nothing that hadn't been munched. All that

was left was the impression of a HUGE set of jagged teeth.

Nobody had a clue what had eaten everything in sight, but they did know three things.

1. It was really MASSIVE.
2. It was really, really HUNGRY.
3. It made them feel really, really, really scared.

Now, fear does strange things to people. It makes them lose their marbles. And it also makes them lose their tempers, even with the people around them they've known and loved for ages. One by one, neighbours started to turn on each other.

'It was you who did this, wasn't it?' Katherine Morgan shouted at Sarah Finigan, despite their families having gone on holiday together for years. 'Revenge for our Matthew lighting the barbecue when you had your washing out two summers back. I knew you were still upset about that!'

Up and down the street, similar arguments were brewing, the atmosphere so thick you needed a chainsaw to cut it.

There was only one family on Storey Street who was neither stressed out, nor fighting with one another. It wasn't a coincidence that this family wasn't even outdoors. The Milners had chosen to watch the chaos unfold from behind their quadruple-glazed windows. (Nothing but the best!)

Masher might not have been able to hear all of the arguments from behind the super-strength panes of glass, but he could see that things were pretty bloomin' tense.

'Blimey, Dad,' he said to Maurice, who stood beside him. 'What's going on out there? They're about to rip each other limb from limb.'

His dad smiled the smile of a fox who'd just been given free rein of a city inhabited solely by chickens.

'Operation: Clear Off, Jessops,' he replied with glee.

'Say what?'

Maurice fixed his son with a look of disappointment.

'We hate them, don't we?'

'Who?'

'Those vagrants next door. The Jessops. They turn up from nowhere and threaten our plan. They refuse our money, offer us dinner, scare us half to death with the contents of that cage, and then that daughter of theirs humiliates you in front of the whole school!'

Masher's cheeks flushed. He found himself incapable of looking Dad in the eye.

'Oh, don't you think I didn't hear about that. There's nothing on this street I don't hear about. Well, no one makes a fool of a

Milner and gets away with it.

'I might be in the sales business, but I'm also a dealer in revenge. I've put a little plan into action. You don't really believe there's a monster on the loose, devouring everything in sight, do you?'

Masher looked back to the chaos in the street. 'Er . . . well . . . look!'

'Masher, Masher, Masher, how many times do I have to tell you. Never let the truth get in the way of a good lie. If there's damp on the wall, paint over it and deny all knowledge. If a house is leaning to one side, say it was designed by the architects of the Leaning Tower of Pisa. If there's a family next door who you desperately want rid of and they happen to have a beast in a cage, make it look like the beast has escaped. Simple.'

Strutting like a peacock who'd just won on a scratch card, Maurice disappeared out of the lounge, only for an almighty roar to erupt from the hallway.

Masher sped into action. Had the beast fought its way inside and wrapped its teeth round his dad's head? Well, he wasn't having that.

But as Masher dashed forwards, picking up the poker from the hearth, the door swung open, and there was a metallic beast that had stepped straight from a sci-fi/horror flick. Its body had been fashioned from the handle of a chainsaw, but its head? Well, it looked like the cybotic cousin of a great white shark, with two rows of hideously sharp teeth – teeth that whirled and swirled as the jaw opened and shut in Masher's direction.

Masher gave a terrified squeal. He felt his bladder weaken, and clamped his knees shut and hoped for the best.

'Don't eat me, don't eat me! I surrender, I'll be your slave!' he yelled.

But just as the metallic beast was about to feast on a starter of bully's head (cooked very, very rare), the engine cut out and Dad's roar cut in instead, as he appeared from behind it.

'For Pete's sake, Masher, MAN UP will you?!'

Masher fought the temptation to curl into a ball and bawl. (Ha! Ball and bawl. Aren't words brilliant?)

'I'm trying, Dad, but this … *thing* was about to amputate my face without anaesthetic.'

'This *thing* is about to frame the Jessops and make our new, super-huge house with plunge pool and cinema room a reality, son.'

'What, by eating everyone on the whole street?' How big did the extension have to be?

'No, you dipstick. Do I look like a sadistic, cold-hearted killer? All I want,' Maurice continued, 'is what is rightfully ours. Or at least what we've rightfully already bribed people for. So it's simple. I got a mate of mine to knock this little beauty together and last night I took it for a walk. Give it another few minutes and a prod in the right direction and those lovely neighbours of ours will be marching straight to that bunch of Jessops demanding answers about what's really in that cage. They'll hound them out for us. This time tomorrow, none of us will even remember they were here and our plan will be back on track.'

As dastardly, evil plans went, it was a good one. Bloomin' good.

'How are we going to frame them then, Dad? I want to help you, plleeeeeease!' Masher begged. He couldn't think of a better way of reminding Jemima and Co. just how powerful he really was.

'Of course you can help. This is your chance to cement our future, while burying that Jessop girl for what she did at school. We'll do it together. It'll be a Milner masterclass in revenge.'

And after hiding their pneumatic beast under the stairs, father and son threw open the front door, to face their unsuspecting victims.

15. Maurice Bares His Teeth

Maurice Milner could sell anything. Ice to the Eskimos, sand to the Arabs. Heck, he was so talented he could flog asthma to a health freak.

So when Maurice burst out of his front door and pasted on his finest look of concern for his fellow man, Masher tried to soak up his dad's performance and learn from it.

'Good grief,' gasped Maurice, as he passed the Christmas's house to see their wheely bin chomped in half. 'My word,' he shouted, as he pointed at the Woodhouses' devoured fence. His concern looked so genuine that Masher had to shove his hands in his pocket to stop himself applauding, before pretending to be horrified himself.

'This is terrible! A tragedy! Something must be done,' he roared, trying to grab as many ears as he could.

'I've called the police,' shouted Dawn Woodhouse from

Number 27.

'We emailed our MP,' yelled Timmy Bentone from Number 37.

'Never mind your MP,' said Maurice. 'This sort of disaster deserves the Prime Minister's attention! These are our homes that have been ravaged. And by what? What sort of crazed beast is in our midst?'

Masher responded to his dad, as if a new, terrifying thought had lodged in his brain. 'But, Dad! What if next time it doesn't stop at our belongings? What if it goes for our pets, or for us?'

A gasp rippled through the crowd, fear spreading like something that spreads really quickly, other than margarine. (Everybody uses that one.)

'It could be a rabid dog!' shouted Dawn Woodhouse.

'Or a wild puma!' yelled Timmy Bentone.

Masher couldn't believe how quickly the hysteria was multiplying. It was dizzying. His head throbbed with the power of it.

'Whatever it is, we should hunt it down and kill it with our bare hands,' called a voice from the back of the crowd, though there wasn't much agreement on this. Tracking it and killing it, especially with bare hands, sounded dangerous and scary, and, well, a bit icky too. Not many folk fancied getting puma entrails stuck beneath their fingernails, regardless of how much they wanted this beast gone.

'Don't panic, my friends,' Maurice said, although he could count the number of friends around him with one finger. Masher. 'I don't think there's any hunting necessary. It's just dawned on me who the perpetrator must be.'

Confused faces stared back. Some were just bemused by his use of the word perpetrator (which is a fancy way of saying 'guilty party').

'It's obvious, isn't it? This is the first time anything like this has ever happened, and some of us have lived here all our lives. Add that fact together with the whopping great cage that sits outside our newest neighbours' caravan, and I think you'll find all the answers you could possibly need!'

Light bulbs pinged on in brains, hands flew to mouths in shock and rage.

'That can't be true, can it? The Jessops seem such lovely people.'

'True, but they are . . . *different* to us, aren't they?'

'And there is a huge cage outside their van.'

'I saw the dad feeding raw meat through the bars the other night. Could be a grizzly bear in there!'

Round and round the rumour mill spun, quicker and quicker, until there was little doubt in anyone's mind that the blame for these monstrous acts of destruction lay with the Jessops. They were so guilty that many people believed they were responsible for other things too, like the Great Fire of London in 1666 and the introduction of sprouts to the country in 1372.

'It's clear we should be talking to the Jessops!' roared Masher, latching onto the paranoia.

His dad agreed. 'I don't wish to point the finger at anyone, but when . . . I mean, *if* they are found to be guilty, they must be made to leave immediately. Or by the end of the month at the very least,' he added under his breath.

As one, the residents of Storey Street marched on The House That Was Stolen, their mood darkening with every step. By the time they reached the caravan, all that was missing from the mob were pitchforks and burning torches. This was a witch-hunt, plain and simple.

'Oi! Jessops!' Masher roared from the picket fence.

No reply.

'I said, OI, JESSOPS!! Get your circus butts out here now! You've a lot of explaining to do. And once you've explained, you'll have a lot of packing to do too!'

Still nothing from the van. Not even a curtain twitched.

'Look how quiet it is in there. That tells us everything we need to know,' shouted Masher to the crowd. 'They're not just thugs and vandals, but cowards as well! Well I'm not having it. Let's arrest them ourselves, starting with whatever's in that cage!'

In a split second, the roaring crowd fell silent. They agreed that something had to be done, but going anywhere near the cage after its inhabitant had eaten most of their prized possessions? Well, they didn't fancy being served up as dessert.

Masher himself was starting to doubt the sanity of the plan, as the beast had begun to emit a low, guttural growl from the shadows. But he couldn't stop, not without losing face, so with teeth knocking and knees chattering (or was it the other way around?), he edged closer still.

'Now listen, you,' he shouted through the bars. 'We don't like what you did overnight. We're peaceful and caring people, and what you did was really, really naughty!'

The crowd looked on nervously. What if the animal didn't like being shouted at? What if the bars weren't as strong as they looked?

It was too nerve-wracking and confusing for most people's timid little heads. They didn't need to worry, though, because just as Masher's hand reached the bars, the caravan door flew open to reveal four Jessops, all yawning and dressed in sequined pyjamas.

'Is there a problem?' Jemima asked, wiping sleepy-dust from her eyes. 'Oh, Masher, don't antagonise little Twinkles. He's really not a morning kind of animal.'

'We know that, don't we?' Masher shouted back, goading the crowd. 'We found that out last night.'

Jemima was confused. Being awoken from her bed by a baying hoard was never her favourite way of starting the day. Not before eating three shredded wheats anyway. Around her, Jacqueline, John-boy and Jeremiah remained sleepy and baffled.

'I'm not surprised you're tired, Jessop,' shouted Masher. 'You and your beast here made quite a night of it, didn't you? Well, letting your pet eat other people's possessions may be the done thing where you come from, but round here, dogs eat from a bowl. They don't devour people's fences or bumpers!'

'Devour what?' Jemima answered, bemused. 'We don't know what you're on about, and I don't see how Twinkles could possibly have done any damage when he's locked in the cage and only I have a key.' From around her neck she pulled a strip of leather, which held a huge key.

'Oh, you think you can smooth-talk your way out of this, don't you? Well you're wrong. Take a look around you. Look what's happened to our property and tell us that your Twinkles here has nothing to do with it.'

Through the gate the Jessops came, walking slowly up the street, eyes widening as the devastation became apparent.

'Oh, this is awful,' whispered Jacqueline, who was as sensitive as her daughter was sparky. She tried to comfort or console people whose prized possessions had been ravaged, but her attempts were met with indifference, or even worse, cold stares and turning backs.

Masher's heart was banging like a draughty toilet door after its owner had beans for tea. It was working. Their plan was working. They believed him!

'Well?' he yelled, once the family had walked the entire length of the street. 'What have you got to say for yourselves? "Sorry" would be a good start. As would a guarantee that you'll be packing up and moving on.'

Jemima looked at her family, their eyes the picture of horror at being so wrongfully framed. But it wasn't a patch on the sadness that scratched at her chest. She turned to Masher, and asked him the simplest of questions.

'Why are you doing this?' she said. 'What have I ever done to you?'

It was a question that stopped Masher momentarily in his tracks, as it made him think. This was a new sensation for him. Not one he liked, but not one he could control either. To make it worse, the only image that popped into his barbed wire brain was a smiling Jemima in the playground, picking him up and carrying him selflessly over the finish line.

'Nghhhh,' he stammered. 'Errrrr.' Why wouldn't his mouth work? Why could he only think of how she'd saved him from humiliation?

He felt the crowd staring at him, wondering why he was doing an impression of an intellectually challenged amoeba.

'Masher, you idiot,' Dad hissed in his ear. 'What are you doing? You've got them on the ropes. Kill! Kill!'

It was enough to shake Masher out of his stupor. Enough for him to spit out his words without having to answer Jemima. 'Open the cage, Jessop.'

Jemima sighed, all of her sadness still aimed at Masher's heart. 'OK. But it's not our fault, any of this mess. And you're about to look silly again. Very silly indeed . . .'

With that, she yanked the leather strap from her neck and

strode towards Twinkles's cage.

The crowd cowered. Masher frowned and crossed his legs in fear.

It looked like Twinkles was about to go walkies . . .

16.

Twinkle, Twinkle, What a Star

Storey Street was throbbing with anticipation and fear.

Jemima Jessop strode purposefully towards the cage door.

'I promise you, Twinkles isn't capable of this kind of destruction,' she said. 'You'll be disappointed by what you find behind these bars.'

'We'll only be disappointed if your thug of an animal isn't brought to justice!' Masher demanded, though he wasn't quite sure how you brought an animal to justice. Slap handcuffs and a prison outfit on it? Put it on trial in a kangaroo court?

He didn't say it out loud, though. He daren't trust his mind to say the right thing, not after the weird and fleeting feelings of guilt he'd experienced.

'Twinkles,' Jemima sang gently. 'Twinky-poo. There are some friends out here to see you, now don't be shy . . .' As she slid the key into the padlock she was met with a roar of Tyrannosauric proportions, so deafening that a gust of wind accompanied it, blowing the hair of each of the assembled throng.

'I've changed my mind,' someone whimpered from the back. 'My car doesn't really need a bonnet. Honest.'

But it was too late to turn back. Seconds after the roar stopped echoing, a pair of green eyes loomed from the darkness, working out who would constitute starters, mains, pudding and cheese course.

Someone screamed and at least seven people broke wind in sheer unadulterated terror. Jemima walked through the cage door, picking up a whip that hung on the wall.

Everyone recoiled, wracked with fear. From within the cage there came a series of piercing roars and howls. After a brief pause that still felt as if it lasted longer than a British summer, Jemima emerged from the darkness, pulling a metal chain, not a bead of sweat on her sweet-looking head.

'Ladies and gentlemen, let me prove to you that our dear pet is no menace. Let me introduce you to the world's most daring dog, Planet Earth's most cunning canine, the galaxy's most marvellous mutt, the one and only TWINKLES!'

With that, the chain went taut and the crowd took a dozen steps back. Maurice hid behind Masher, Danny Christmas said a little prayer. But no one, not even the resident clairvoyant, Mystic Margaret, could've predicted what happened next.

Instead of a prowling rabid beast, with the jaws of a great white shark, what emerged from the cage was the world's biggest multi-coloured beach ball, and standing on top of it, on its hind legs, was a teeny-tiny doggie. At least these ageing eyes of mine thought it was a dog.

It could've been, at first glance, a rat on a lead. Either way, it was small, the sort of dog that annoying pop stars carry around in their handbags instead of a lipstick or their dignity.

Fear turned quickly into confusion. Masher looked up at his dad, whose face told a story, and the story read:

Once there was a plan. A really good, devious dastardly plan. But then the plan turned into the Titanic and started sinking quickly . . .

You see, there was no way in the world that dear old Twinkles could've bitten off the trunk of an oak tree, or the bonnet of a car. Dear old Twinkles would have to dislocate his jaw to fit the smallest bone in his gob. And besides, he was way more interested in entertaining the masses than devouring the children on Storey Street. Round and round the front garden he spun, balancing on top of the ball, like a . . . well, like a small dog

on top of a beach ball. To add to the complexity of the moves, Jemima tossed him tennis balls, which he balanced one by one on top of his nose, before flicking them away. (You weren't expecting him to juggle them, were you? He's a DOG, for goodness' sake.)

Nobody knew what to make of it. Sure, they were being entertained, but this didn't change the fact that many of their belongings had been mangled or devoured, and it was clear this dog wasn't to blame. He was way too cute.

'This can't be right,' wailed Masher. 'There must be another animal in that cage. It must be asleep or drugged. You've all heard it, just like me!'

To be honest, he did have a point. How could that roar come from that tiny mouth? How could those piercing green eyes belong to Twinkles?

A few confused voices lent Masher their support, who marched with his dad towards the cage, only to be stopped by Jemima.

'You don't need to look in there, do you?' she said.

'I think we do,' the bully answered. 'If you're hiding more secrets, then we need to know about them!'

'OK,' she sighed, standing aside. 'Though I promise, you won't find any other animals.'

Into the cage ploughed Masher and Maurice, the braver members of the crowd tentatively moving closer too. Using the torches on their phones, the Milners threw light to all four corners of the cage, but they found no slumbering beast. What they did find was the hugest magnifying glass ever manufactured. Sitting half a metre back from the bars, just where the darkness began, it stretched the entire length of the enclosure, and when Masher stepped behind it he became even more muscly and 'Masher-ish' than usual. He looked mahoosive!

'You see,' Jemima sighed, 'The best illusions are the best illusions because they are the best *illusions*.'

Masher looked at her as if she was speaking Swahili. (I was a bit confused too, to be honest.)

'We've performed all over the world. In places far more dangerous than this. Sometimes, believe it or not, people thought we were strange and not to be trusted. They would threaten us. Can you believe that?'

She raised her left eyebrow at Masher.

'So we rigged up this contraption to magnify Twinkles a little, to make more of his shadow and piercing emerald eyes.' Right on cue, from on top of his ball, Twinkles beamed and seemed to wink at the crowd. 'That way we could ensure people wouldn't carry out their threats. But I can see now that we've scared you. And I'm sorry about that. Really I am.'

Jemima offered her hand in the ultimate act of peace. Masher stared at it, feeling the tiniest of tingles in his fingers, before ignoring it and turning them back into fists. He looked around the magnifying glass, part-hating, part-admiring just how ingenious the Jessops had been.

Behind the magnifying glass was a living space fit for the Dog King of Scandinavia. Not only was there a double bed with silk sheets and plump pillows, a leather settee and back-scratching pole, but also a machine that would lick Twinkle's bum for him, to save him the bother.

Masher's mouth fell open. It was better than his own room – not that he wanted that machine, honest.

'It's a lovely space, isn't it?' said Jemima. 'I felt so guilty about making him sleep outside that I wanted it to be super comfy.'

On and on Masher's eyes roved, spotting even more details. Above him, he spotted the other part of the jigsaw: a small microphone that hung from the ceiling.

'That's a voice-altering mike,' said Jemima. 'It turns the most normal voice like mine' – she stepped underneath the mike – 'into a terrifying, blood-curdling yowl.' The change in her voice was extraordinary. It was like the devil himself had been gargling with broken glass and was speaking to Masher directly. 'Twinkles doesn't exactly have the roar of a tiger, do you, boy?' she asked the dog, who replied with a yap no louder than a doorbell that's batteries are running perilously low.

She'd thought of everything, Masher fumed. All this detail made his dad's plan look . . . amateurish, and he'd never dreamed anyone was capable of that.

All he could do was stomp out of the cage with his dad, twitching as the Jessops addressed the crowd.

'I hope our little magic trick here hasn't disturbed you too much,' offered Jacqueline, 'but you can see too that it simply couldn't be Twinkles who caused this damage. He doesn't have it in him.'

Twinkles seemed to smile sweetly once more, before cocking his leg on the gatepost.

'We feel terrible that our caravan seems to be the only house unaffected by this strange phenomenon, so please let us help put things straight. We can paint, saw, repair – anything to make things normal again.'

Now the people of Storey Street might have been naïve and easily led by the likes of the Milners, but they were also big of heart. Satisfied that Twinkles was not a T-rex, they took the Jessops up on their offer of assistance.

Not so keen to oblige were Masher and Maurice, who slunk away, father swearing and spitting, son wondering just how far his dad would now go to win the war.

Jemima watched, smiling sadly, as she turned to Danny Christmas.

'Mum was wrong about something, you know. Our van wasn't the only place not to be attacked. Look. The Milners' mansion is spotless.'

Danny's mouth fell open. 'And doesn't that make you

suspicious?'

'Of course.'

Their heads were suddenly full of warning signs.

'It has to be them who created this mess,' sighed Jemima. 'I don't know how, but it has to be, doesn't it?'

'Then we have to speak out. Point the finger, just like they did at you.' Danny started to clear his throat, ready to expose Masher and his family for the conniving vagabonds that they were.

Jemima pulled Danny's hands down at his sides, before looking back to Masher.

The bully had reached his front door and was looking at them too. He didn't like the way Christmas and the circus girl were staring. They knew too much, and what made it worse was that she was getting inside his head. He didn't know how she was doing it. His brain was a cluttered and dusty place, but somehow she'd found a key and had invited herself in.

He wasn't going to have it. No one told him what to do. He was Masher Milner. OK, they might have lost this battle, but there was no way he or Dad would let them lose the war. They would come again, and next time, the gloves would be well and truly off.

17. When Two Tribes Go to War

Jemima and Danny kept schtum about their suspicions, their lips tighter than a cyclist's underpants. But they knew the Milners were responsible for whatever had got the munchies that night in Storey Street.

Masher knew that Jemima knew too. He watched her and Danny, saw them whispering together in the corner of the playground. What he couldn't work out was, if they knew he and his dad had been up to no good, why hadn't they dobbed them in? And why, when the Milners hated the Jessops so openly, had Jemima helped him out?

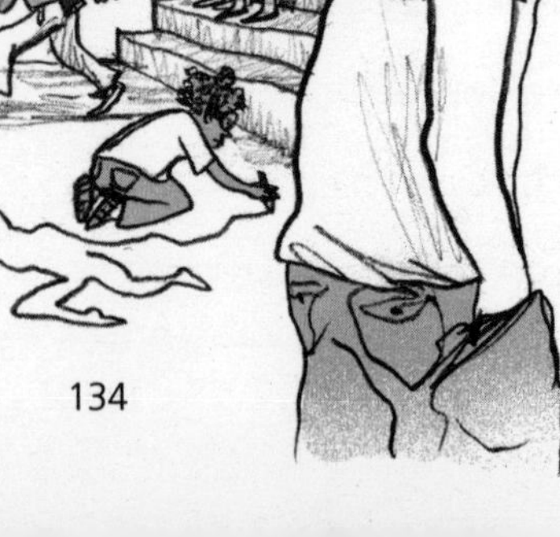

His mind kept flashing back to the race in the playground. Who did she think she was, walking about with her random acts of kindness? It made him angry enough to want to chop down trees with his bare hands. Well, he wouldn't let it rub off on him. He wouldn't. No way.

Jemima could give him the best present in the world, a pair of boots with built-in bazookas, and it still wouldn't turn him soft. His dad needed the Jessops gone, so that was what was going to happen. The Milners were Seacross royalty, and when you're royalty you can do whatever you chuffing want.

Masher threw every thought he had into helping Dad come up with a new plan of mass destruction. Except Dad didn't seem too interested in Masher joining him.

To say it was tense at Milner Mansions would be a massive understatement, like saying that eating asparagus makes your wee smell a little bit. It was like a war zone. (Their house, not your loo after an asparagus tinkle.)

Dad prowled around the house for days, growling and harrumphing and doing his best impression of a bear with a hangover.

'Seven and a half big ones that machine cost me,' he moaned. 'Now what am I going to do with it? It's not like I can use it to cut the grass.'

Masher stomped around behind him, copying his every move and grimace, but it only served to earn him a rebuke and a sore ear.

That said, Maurice Milner was not a man to sit and mope. You didn't become the most successful estate agent in Seacross history without the ability to come up with a Plan B. Maurice called in his finest minds from work, including one salesman who'd just sold a garden shed with no roof as a 'convertible house – perfect for those who want to invite the outside in!'

Eight of them arrived at nine o'clock one morning and sat around the kitchen table, before Dad closed the door, leaving Masher (to his great distress) in the hallway.

Well, Masher didn't know what to make of this. At first he thought it was a mistake, but on entering the room with a notebook, pen and packet of Bourbon biscuits, was told:

'Get the fl*&%$£@£$p out, Masher. When we need a cup of tea, we'll tell you!'

Out he slunk, deflated. What had Dad meant? Surely if they were going to come up with something watertight, they'd need his help? He'd seen the Jessops up close and personal. Witnessed just how devious they could be. But at the same time Dad's eyes had burned with a fire that he didn't want to play with. Not even with oven gloves.

Instead, he snivelled and sat with his ear to the door, straining to hear the plan take shape. Not that he could hear much, apart from lots of evil laughter, and if he wasn't mistaken, his name being mentioned repeatedly.

Was that his cue to go in again? He wanted to, but daren't.

No matter how hard he listened, even when he tried to shove his lughole inside the keyhole, he couldn't make out why he kept being mentioned.

All he could do was wait, and see how he could contribute to the new plan. Whatever they wanted of him, he'd deliver the goods. He'd show Dad how much he needed him.

The mood next door, chez Jessop, should've been far happier, but when Danny Christmas found Jemima leaning on the picket fence on the way to school, her face was long and frowny.

'What's up?' Danny asked, worried. The frown didn't suit

Jemima. It sat on her face like a moustache on a beauty queen.

'Nothing,' she answered. 'Don't worry about it.'

But Danny was worried. Jemima had brought not just sunshine, but a whole bloomin' rainbow into their lives and he didn't like seeing her blue.

So he tried again. 'Come on. Whatever it is, it can't be as bad as the time I managed to wedge a pencil sharpener up my nose by accident.'

Jemima stared at him, no sign of a smile.

'Seriously,' he went on. 'It was a nightmare having kids endlessly shoving pencils up my hooter.'

Still nothing.

'Mind you, when I sneezed I fired the sharpest bogies known to man. Like bullets they were. The army wanted to make me their secret weapon.'

Finally, a smirk, which made Danny laugh too.

'You are a plank, Danny Christmas.'

'Maybe, but I'm a plank who made you laugh, finally. So what's going on?'

'Oh, stuff at home.'

'Like what?'

Jemima exhaled noisily. 'Mum and Dad are wondering if we've

done the right thing, stopping here.'

Danny didn't like the sound of that. His heart threatened to race, stop and break simultaneously.

''Course they have.' It wasn't much of an argument, but it was all he had.

'You say that, but we've been in this position before . . . more than once.'

'But you've only just arrived. It'll be fine in time.'

'You reckon? We've stayed places a lot shorter. Eighteen minutes and thirty-two seconds is the record.'

'Blimey.' Danny tried to work out how that must feel. 'That's rubbish.'

'That's an understatement.'

'It'll get better here, I promise. It's only Masher rocking the boat.'

'Mum and Dad were talking about that whole beast thing last night when they thought I was in bed. Mum's really upset about what went on. That people thought we would allow Twinkles to destroy their stuff. That we're nothing more than a bunch of wild animals.'

'People are quick to jump to conclusions, but you know, you do have a HUGE cage outside your caravan.'

'For good reason. Some places, the second we pitch up, people say stuff and throw stuff. They paint words on the side of the van. Words so horrible, even after Dad's painted over it we can all still see them.'

'People aren't like that around here.' Danny dropped the volume in his voice, 'Not apart from them next door.'

Jemima wasn't so sure. 'People might know Twinkles didn't eat their stuff, but they still won't trust us. Not really. Just watch. They'll be different, not as friendly. Mum and Dad reckon it's just a matter of time before something happens again.'

'Do you think Masher and his dad are plotting again?'

Jemima gave him a look that said, DUH, REALLY? And Danny knew she was right. Of course they were.

'Do you want me to talk to your parents? Tell them how brilliant living here is?'

Jemima shook her head sadly. 'No point. We've been in this situation a million times before. They're stubborn. It's our middle name.'

And that was it. Conversation over. But as Jemima trudged towards the school gates, it dawned on her just how much she liked it here – the school, Danny, the whole blinking lot.

And at that moment she felt something surge through her

body, a new level of determination.

Here she was, living on a cool street, with a cool friend who liked her a lot. It felt great that their caravan wheels hadn't turned once in weeks. And she wasn't going to let Masher change that.

Jemima pulled herself tall, puffed out her chest and stared determinedly at her enemy's house.

Masher might want a war, but she wouldn't sink to his level.

Despite her fears about the future, she'd try to win him over in her own way. The Jessop way.

18. Light Fingers and Heavy Hearts

A week before the Milners' builders were due to arrive, things started to go missing on Storey Street. They were small at first.

'Here!' said Dennis Gee from Number 43. 'Someone's had it away with our letterbox!'

'You should think yourself lucky,' answered Mickey Wragg who lived next door. 'Some toerag has pinched our licence plate, and our wheely bin!'

Naturally, this pricked the ears of our heroes, Jemima and Danny, who were walking by. As they plodded up the street, they heard similar tales of unusual thefts: licence plates, window boxes, wheely bins, all stolen.

Not exactly high-value items, but the sorts of thefts that didn't go unnoticed, especially when Storey Street's residents were still confused by the unsolved 'mystery' of the beast that had roamed among them.

But while people scratched their heads and made more visits to the DIY shop, Jemima went into high alert.

'This is it,' Jemima whispered to Danny. 'This is how they try and get their claws into us again.'

'Could just be kids messing about.'

'Nah, this stinks of Milner. Can't you smell it?'

Danny lifted his head and sniffed. There was an aroma of egginess in the air, but he'd put that down to the missing bins being replaced by black bags on the pavement, a few of which had already been ripped open by grateful foxes.

'So what do we do?' he asked.

'We click into surveillance mode. We monitor Masher every second of the day, keep a minute-by-minute log, note when he eats, sleeps, burps, everything. If I'm right, more stuff's going to go missing, and when it does, we have to have it out with him before it's too late.'

As plans go, it wasn't the best. The last person to negotiate with Masher ended up with a nose shaped like a parrot's beak and the worst wedgie known to man. But as it was the only plan they had, they had to run with it.

And actually, they were wise to wait to speak to Masher, because until the next paragraph, the bully was also clueless, both about the thefts going on under his nose, and who was responsible.

Only when he was finally summoned to the war chamber (the kitchen) did he realise the depths of deviousness his dad would sink to. Honestly, they were so low Maurice Milner should've been a scuba-diving limbo dancer who lived in a subterranean bungalow.

'Masher, my boy!' Maurice beamed in front of his team of devious dealers. He said it with such warmth that Masher was confused. How could Dad ignore him for days and then speak to him like this? 'That Jessop girl. You hate her, don't you?'

Blimey, thought Masher. That was some question to start with. And one he should know the answer to immediately. Of course he hated her. Because she was so clever. And sparky. And friendly. And because his dad had told him he should.

'Well?' Dad barked. 'Do you hate her or not? Are you in or are you out?'

This was no time to hesitate. Dad wasn't talking about belly buttons. Masher couldn't be out. He wouldn't disappoint his dad.

'I'm in,' he said. 'I . . . hate her.' Though, in all honesty, he didn't really know what that word meant.

'Good,' Dad continued. 'Hate is good. It keeps you on your

toes. And you'll need to be alert, boy. As it's you, ultimately, who is going get rid of her and her weirdo family for ever. Exciting, eh.'

You might expect there to be a question mark at the end of that last sentence, but it isn't a grammatical mistake, as Maurice wasn't asking a question. He was telling Masher.

Masher nodded, though his head movements were smaller, less certain than normal. For some reason, instead of being excited about Dad's plan, he was nervous.

'Excellent. Because lately, you've been a bit of a wimp, and how can I possibly groom you to take over the family business when you've got less backbone than an agoraphobic jellyfish?'

Masher had no idea what an agora-wotsit was, but he knew it wasn't good. And he knew that the words stung like a jellyfish. Why would his dad say that when he'd always done everything he could to be just like him? He had to show him, to prove to him he was a chip off the abrasive block.

'Tell me what I need to do, Dad.'

'It's simple,' Maurice said, leading Masher out of the front door towards the shed in the yard.

'We've four days left until the diggers arrive, and there's no sign of the Jessops slinging their hook. And should they dig their heels in, I don't trust our mayor to help us evict them, despite what I paid him. So me and the team here—' Dad's cronies smiled their most twisted evil grins as he unlocked the shed '—have been running a plan that really will turn everyone against these circus rejects.'

Maurice paused dramatically, checking there were no unwanted ears waggling in their direction.

'For the last three days, they've been making stuff disappear. Nothing valuable, nothing treasured, but enough to be noticed.'

With a finger to his lips, Maurice lifted the corner of a tarpaulin in the shed, to reveal the most useless array of stolen knick-knacks. It was like being dragged to the worst jumble sale in the world. Whipping the tarp back into position, on Dad went.

'Now, I know Plan A didn't exactly pay off, but it sowed a seed, a seed that the Jessops are strange, and not to be trusted. I mean, all that business with magnifying glasses and microphones! So I'm going to water that seed. For the next three days the team here will continue, taking bigger and bigger stuff, until on the night of the deadline . . . well, that's where you come in. That's your moment to shine, when you truly show yourself as a Milner.'

This sort of challenge from his dad was the sort Masher normally rose to. To be like his dad was usually all the carrot Masher needed.

So why was he suddenly nervous at the prospect? He tried to think of something to say, but didn't trust his lips to convey the message properly. Instead he grinned menacingly, hoping he didn't, in fact, look constipated.

'We've thought long and hard about one ultimate object that we could take, that would have everyone on the street up in arms. And we've found it. All you have to do now, son, is be the one to do the deed and take it.'

Masher gulped, his Adam's apple suddenly the size of a beach ball. What was Dad asking him to do? What was it that needed taking?

'That boy in your class, Elliot Tipps. The one with a rubbish footballer for a dad. You know the one, don't you?'

Masher nodded. He didn't have to steal Elliot's dad, did he? Because, to be honest, he didn't want to. It wasn't in his job description or his name. He was a Masher, not a kidnapper. Not that he said this, of course. He didn't have a death wish.

'It turns out that fifteen years ago Elliot's dad won the FA cup, before his career went predictably down the pan.' Maurice didn't like anyone even remotely successful, even if it was over a decade ago. 'His winners' medal is his pride and joy. I'm told it sits on his bedside table, where the idiot kisses it every night before going to sleep. Worth a pretty penny too, apparently. More than anything else these losers own.'

Masher might not have been the smartest, but he knew where this was heading.

'Well, imagine the racket he'd make if it was to go missing. Imagine the reaction of the whole street if their favourite footballer had his precious medally-wedally stolen. So all you have to do, my boy, being the smallest person on our team, is sneak in through their top bedroom window and swipe that medal for me.'

Masher stomach lurched like someone had just fed him a bird muck sarnie.

'Is that a-a-all?' he stuttered. 'And w-w-what are we going to do with it then?'

Maurice grinned. 'We're going to dump it with all the other stuff we've lifted, in that cage next door. And when the police arrive, they'll find it, arrest the Jessops and tow away their van. That way they can't steal our house, can they?'

Masher felt dizzy. As if his dad was shaking him upside down by his boots instead of just talking to him. He didn't understand why he felt weird like this. He'd spent his life watching his dad's dodgy deals, and had done nothing but applaud and feel massively proud.

But this? This plan was different. This time he was properly involved and he felt like a wooden tent pole being hammered into a concrete block. The prospect of such thievery just to frame someone, well, it didn't sit right. It sort of hurt, but not as much as the hurt his dad would inflict if Masher were to say no.

What was he going to d—

'Masher? Masher! Are you listening to me, son? For Pete's sake, now is not the time for you to zone out.'

'But what if someone caught me? What if they called the cops? I mean, it's breaking and entering isn't it, as well as . . . you know . . . stealing?'

Maurice shook his head. What had he done to raise such a wimp of a boy? Then again, this would be the making of him. 'It's only stealing if they don't get it back. And they will, because the police will find it in that rat's cage. All you're doing is borrowing it.'

Masher chewed that fact over his in his teeny-tiny brain. It rolled around like a pea on the world's biggest roulette wheel.

Maurice felt his temperature rise at his son's indecision. 'Have you lost your nerve or something? Forgotten who you are? The Tippses always leave their top window open. You're not breaking into anything. All you have to do is shimmy up the drainpipe and squeeze through the gap. In and out in thirty seconds. Imagine the glory. It'll be something to tell your kids, your grandkids even. I know I'll be talking about my brave, intrepid son until the day I die.'

And with that, Maurice Milner did something strange. Something he'd never done in his whole life. He hugged his son. Not a headlock or a choke hold, but a genuine cuddle. Well, I say 'genuine'. Maurice Milner wouldn't know genuine if you gave him a dictionary bookmarked on that page. He was doing it because he needed his son to say yes, and he was bored of terrorising him to get his own way.

It was effective too, as the hug was all Masher needed to cave in like a squirrel in an acorn shop.

His dad needed him. Needed. Him. How could he possibly say no?

The word 'morals' faded from his mind.

'OK, Dad . . . I'll do it.'

His voice might've sounded firm, but inside he was crumbling, like an old, stale biscuit.

19.

Jessops Never Say Die

Three days edged past.

Seventy-two hours.

Four thousand, three hundred and twenty minutes.

Two hundred and fifty nine thousand, two hundred seconds.

Enough time for me to grow a beard down to my knees, and more than enough time for Jemima Jessop to worry herself silly.

Because within those three days, more stuff went missing. Doorbells, then doors. Bike pumps, then bikes, apples, then trees. Each theft got bigger, leaving the residents of Storey Street more nervous and increasingly paranoid.

Jemima and Danny monitored every step Masher and his dad made, filling four notebooks and wearing out fifteen pencils. Their eyes were more peeled than a bunch of ripe bananas in the hands of a ravenous chimp, but they saw nothing. Well, nothing apart from Maurice's grin stretch wider and wider, so wide that soon it wouldn't just be their house extension they'd need planning permission for.

But as smug as Maurice looked, they couldn't find any evidence of wrongdoing, either from him or his son, whose mood, strangely, didn't quite match his dad's. His thuggery levels seemed dampened, his fists not as clenched as they usually were. He hadn't walloped anyone in days.

'Something is definitely going on,' Jemima mused. 'Either that or he's become the world's first living brain donor.'

'Maybe you were wrong,' Danny answered. 'Maybe he isn't up to anything at all.'

'I'd like to believe that. It might help Mum and Dad feel differently about this place.' Her brain didn't believe it, though. She was still really, truly fed up about their chances of moving on, yet again.

Just as the fear threatened to nibble away at her vital organs, Jemima pulled herself back into line and took a deep, deep breath.

Hang on a cotton-picking minute, she shouted at herself. This wasn't how it worked. She was a Jessop. And Jessops never said 'die'. It wasn't in their dictionary.

Jemima sprinted to the corner shop, bought a dozen more

notebooks and a box of pencils and doubled her efforts; she'd interrogate the local stray cat if she thought it'd give her the lowdown on what Masher might be doing.

She even convinced Danny to help her set up a surveillance post in his bedroom with a notebook, binoculars and telescope, plus walkie-talkies connected straight to her van.

'We'll stay up all night, if need be,' she said optimistically.

'I normally go to bed at nine,' Danny answered. 'My mum says I'm a nightmare if I don't get ten solid hours.'

Jemima refused to be deflated by this, even when they realised that while setting up the surveillance, someone had stolen Jack Boo's skateboard, a gnome from Kay Catt's garden, and the dignity of a strange old man who lived at Number 67, who for some reason was dressed like a wizard.

'Hm, interesting,' Jemima said. 'Things are going missing every hour now instead of every day. How long until it's every minute? And how long till they pin it on us?'

Jemima, to her credit, refused to get wound up, and instead practised hard on her unicycle, while juggling AND spying on the Milners. Her nerves were tattered, but as it turned out, her tummy wasn't the only one imitating a cement mixer.

Her arch-enemy's guts were also going ten to the dozen, though Masher's answer was to try and eat away his nerves. Two pizzas, three chicken legs, three rounds of toast and a bunch of grapes had made their way down his gullet since lunchtime, and he still felt hungry.

His mission shouldn't have bothered him; if anything it was what he'd been building towards ever since he Mashed an avocado at the age of seven months. Now, with the ultimate accolade of his dad's pride almost in his grasp, well, it all felt strangely beyond him.

'Come on, Masher, pull yourself together,' he grimaced, slapping his palm against his forehead, killing more precious brain cells. 'It's not stealing, it's borrowing. And it's borrowing for all the right reasons.' But no matter how many times he repeated it, he saw Jemima's face in his head, telling him it was wrong to steal.

What he needed was something to focus his brain, and he got it in the shape of what his dad called a 'love tap' to the back of his head. Masher lurched forward. The 'love tap' was more like a full-blooded slap to anyone else.

'You nearly ready, boy?' Maurice asked.

'Uh-huh . . .' Masher squeaked, sounding as if he'd been inhaling helium non-stop for the last hundred and thirty-seven days.

'Good. There's one hour and thirty-three minutes till the sun sets. Between now and then more stuff is going to go walkies, just to really whip up the fear round here. The second the sun goes sleepy-bo-bos, I want you up that drainpipe quicker than a rat up a . . . drainpipe.'

It wasn't the most imaginative analogy, and certainly not the most motivating, but it didn't matter. Maurice had inspired his employees for years through pure, undiluted fear.

'Don't let me down now, you hear? The medal is the key to us pulling this plan off, and you're the only one in Team Milner small enough to get through that window. Succeed, then glory and a much bigger bedroom await. Fail, and . . . well, it'll be painful for all of us, you included. You do want to please your old dad, the man who brought you up, don't you?'

Masher gulped, his throat more parched than a tumble dryer full of sand. He watched as his dad backed away, not breaking eye contact until he reached the door.

Masher tried one last time to make himself look tough, even though he felt anything but. Raising his fists, he cracked his knuckles menacingly, then flinched when he bent one finger too far back for comfort.

Why, all of a sudden, was being tough, so . . . well . . . tough?

20.

The Sun Has Got its Hat On

The sun had had a hard day.

But tonight, it didn't want to finish work; it wanted to stay up and watch what happened on Storey Street. But if it did, there would be no cover of darkness for Masher to sneak around under, so frankly I had to have strong words, and tell it that if it didn't go to bed, this story would never finish, and there would be millions, no, squazillions, of disappointed readers (OK . . . at least three) all pointing the finger in its direction.

So, after a promise that I would tell it the rest in the morning, the sun agreed to set, and grumpily sank behind the hills, which allows us to get on with the story. Now, let me see . . .

Storey Street was rife with theft and pilfery. Items were disappearing at a ridiculous rate. Rose bushes, fountains and rolls of turf from gardens; mirrors, fluffy dice and nodding dogs from cars; chimney pots, doorbells and numbers from houses. To the street's residents there was no rhyme or reason to the thefts, no logic as to why such a skilled burglar would want such random items, but it infuriated folk enough to set tongues wagging about who might be responsible.

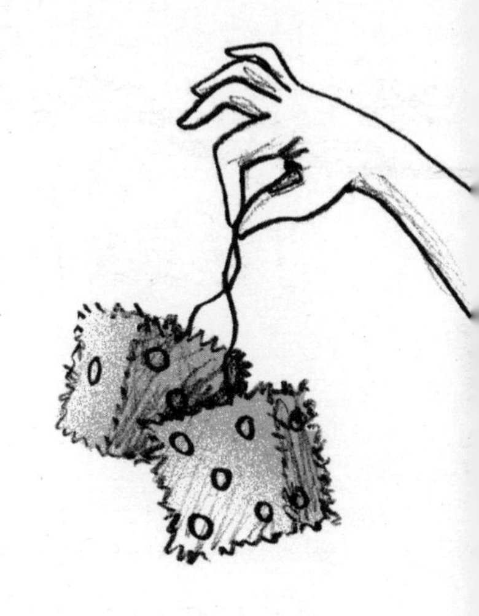

'Anyone seen anybody matching the description of a robber? Stripy jumper, mask, bag marked "swag"?' asked Willy Winklebum from Number 21.

'No,' answered his wife, Wanda. 'But there was a van parked up earlier that I didn't recognise . . .'

'Oh, don't be so flipping ridiculous. It's obvious, isn't it?' interrupted a man no one recognised (though he was dressed smartly, like an estate agent). 'If you want to find who's responsible, you only need look in one direction.' And he looked in one direction (no, not towards the boy band), the direction of the Jessops's caravan, before disappearing as quickly as he had arrived.

From his bedroom window, Masher Milner watched events unfold.

His face was covered in camouflage paint, though he was feeling so queasy he doubted he needed it. His heart hammered, his palms sweated. He thought he might be sick at any given moment. But he swallowed both the nerves and the puke when he heard a knock at the door and his dad's face appeared.

'It's time, son,' Maurice whispered. 'Go on. Make your daddy proud.'

Storey Street was quiet. Quieter than a group of librarians on a meditation holiday. Yep, it was that quiet.

The only sound was the occasional clink of a padlock, as residents secured their most prized possessions from the thief in their midst before going inside for the night.

Pretty much everything left outside the houses was under lock and key; even some padlocks had been chained up.

On seeing this, Masher's heart leaped. Surely this level of

security would put his mission uncontrollably beyond him? He couldn't help but hope so.

Creeping stealthily along the shadows, he trained his eyes on Elliot's dad's bedroom window, the home of his prized footie medal.

Please be closed, please be closed, please be closed, he thought. But as his eyes focused through the gloom, he saw the top window teasingly ajar, just beside the drainpipe. There was no way out of it. He had to go on. So go on he did, cajoling himself, telling himself again and again that it was borrowing not stealing, borrowing not stealing, borrowing, not stealing.

Masher skipped away from lights that shone from living rooms and television screens. He even evaded a pair of eyes pressed tightly to a pair of binoculars from a nearby upstairs window.

The eyes did belong to someone by the way; they weren't just two random eyeballs sitting on their own in a glass jar. There weren't any mad scientists living on Storey Street, not ones that appear in this particular story anyway.

These eyes were planted firmly in the head of Jemima Jessop, who, along with Danny Christmas (after begging his parents for a sleepover), had sworn not to sleep until they brought Masher to justice, even if that meant staying up all night.

That was the plan, anyway, but in practice it had been a long day, full of energy-sapping anxiety, before Danny's mum had fed them both a massive chippy tea, which had left them feeling full and sleepy. In fact, as Masher swept past his vantage point, Danny was on the bed, burping in his sleep, while Jemima's eyes were threatening to close . . .

'ALL THINGS BRIGHT AND BEAUTIFUL!!' sang a tuneless voice from downstairs. It was Danny's dad, Father Christmas (chortle), brushing up on his hymns before Sunday's service. Thank goodness, thought Jemima. His voice was so tuneless in the chorus it was impossible to sleep through.

Seconds passed, a verse saw the room fall quiet, leaving Jemima's eyelids to sag once more . . .

'ALL CREATURES GREAT AND SMALL . . .'

She was upright again, cursing herself for feeling so tired when there was so much at risk . . . but she couldn't help it, she was so tir—

'ALL THINGS WISE AND WONDERFUL . . .'

Her eyes were stinging, as if she'd been attacked by wasps. So tired . . . so tired . . . that even the caterwauling from downstairs wasn't quite enough, her vision fading one last . . . final . . . time . . .

'THE LORD GOD MAAAAAADE THEM AAAAAAAALL!'

The volume was so loud it knocked Jemima off her stool, and as she embarrassedly jumped to her feet, she swore she spotted something up the street. Maybe it was divine intervention care of Danny's dad's singing, maybe not, but there was definitely someone down there. A single shadowy figure, tinged with green, so green they were either:

A. covered in camouflage paint

or

B. about to throw up

Either way, Jemima knew this was the moment she'd been waiting for. Without pausing to even offer a prayer of thanks, she shook Danny awake, belted down the stairs and crashed into the darkness of Storey Street.

21.

Incey Wincey Milner Climbing up the Pipe

Masher had never realised he was terrified of heights, until now. He was used to looking down on people, but that didn't normally scare him – if anything it made him feel phenomenally powerful. But here, five metres off the ground and still not within reach of the bedroom window, he didn't feel so tough.

He was scared of falling, scared of being caught, scared of getting stuck, scared of failing, there were so many fears jostling for position that it was a wonder his brain managed to keep his limbs moving at all.

'It'll be OK, it'll be OK, it'll be OK,' he repeated out loud, reminding himself that he'd seen the family go out earlier in the evening, and that they had no pet to attack him. Apart from a fish, and unless they'd traded a tiddler for a piranha that managed to live outside of water, then he reckoned he'd be all right.

Focusing his mind, Masher pulled himself up past the window ledge, until he could step upon it. Then, with a surprisingly deft movement for a boy of his bulk, he levered his arms and head through the window, panicking slightly that the opening wouldn't be wide enough to accommodate his chest. Breathing in, his upper body found a way through, unlike the belt loop of his jeans, which managed to snag on the window lever, leaving him dangling upside down.

This did little for his anxiety, as you can imagine. *Oh no!* he wailed inwardly. *Please don't let Dad be watching this!*

On he struggled, legs thrashing so wildly outside the window that he might as well have attached a white flag to his ankles, with a message that shouted, 'Coo-eee, Mr Policeman, come and get me!!'

It certainly didn't go unnoticed by Danny and Jemima, who were now tearing down Storey Street in hot pursuit. Or at least, Jemima was. Danny had suddenly stopped dead.

'Hang on!' he yelled. 'What are we doing?'

Jemima paused. 'What do you mean? We're stopping Masher, aren't we?'

'But why are we doing it? Isn't that what the police get paid for?'

Danny was right. 'Course he was. It's never the brightest idea to follow a burglar into an empty building. Have-a-go heroes often come complete with broken noses and black eyes. But that didn't bother Jemima. Not a bit.

'We can't go to the police. If they caught Masher they'd lock him up.'

'Er . . . yeah?' Danny answered, confused. 'That's how justice works. Burgle a house, get locked up. Sounds fair to me.'

Jemima looked at Danny as if he was the village idiot. 'Do you really think Masher wants to do this?'

'He's doing a pretty good impression of it ... apart from the crazy leg dancing.'

'Well, I'm telling you he doesn't. He's only doing it because he's unhap—'

'Enough with the "he's unhappy" thing. I didn't understand it before, and I certainly don't understand it now. He's doing it because he's a vindictive nutter who wants to drive you out of your house before buying everybody else's!'

'Do you really believe that?' Jemima asked.

Danny nodded forcefully.

'More than you trust me?'

Danny nodded, then shook his head, then nodded again. His neck felt confused. And sore.

'I'm telling you, Danny, we can sort this without the police. It'll be better for you, better for me, and better for that wally up there too. So let's try, please?'

Danny didn't like it, not a bit, but Jemima was looking at him so pleadingly that he didn't know what else to do. 'OK, but if we get nowhere, we call the police, yes?'

'You can even use my phone,' she answered, before whispering under her breath, 'Well, you could if I had one . . .'

On they ran. Then, as they neared Elliot's house, Jemima banked right and crossed the road, away from the scene of the crime.

'Where are you going?' Danny panted.

'Shortcut. If you want to follow, take the conventional route.'

Shortcut? Danny thought. How could running in the other direction possibly be a shortcut? But he didn't have time to Google it, so he watched as Jemima effortlessly scaled the telegraph pole opposite the Tippses' residence.

As she climbed, Jemima glanced towards Masher. He seemed to have resorted to emergency measures, wrestling his jeans open and off, before sliding with an almighty thump to the floor beyond, his Y-fronts a dazzling white as they flashed past the window. She expected to see Masher reappear and grab his jeans, but instead they hung there like an ill-fitting curtain.

Jemima turned her attention to the telephone wire, which she danced her way across. There was a grace to her movements that most people never managed on the ground, never mind three storeys up. She bounded across the line in what seemed to be a dozen steps, while below, a more reluctant Danny started to hoist his way up the drainpipe.

Only when she reached the bedroom window did Jemima pause. Was she doing the right thing? Was she even right about Masher? It wasn't like her to doubt herself, but for once she couldn't help it.

What would he do when she confronted him? Would he raise his fists if she thwarted whatever evil plan he had? Would she even manage to get him to put his jeans back on?

These terrifying thoughts invaded Jemima's head, until she remembered everything that was at stake. Then, and only then, did she propel herself forward, straight into the Masher's path.

22.

Jemima Deserves a Medal

It didn't take Masher long to locate the booty. You didn't win an FA cup medal and hide it under a bushel. Besides, no one in the Tipps family even knew what a bushel was. Come to think of it, neither do I. Is it some kind of shrub?

Anyway, Elliot's dad had no interest in bushels or their meaning. Instead he kept his medal on his bedside table, so he could see it as soon as he opened in eyes in the morning. Wouldn't you do the same?

Masher eyed the well-polished prize carefully, nervous to touch it. Once he'd done that, it would feel like there was no way back.

Even at night the medal shone, the glare from a streetlight bouncing off its mirror-like surface. So reflective was it that for a moment Masher thought he spotted someone else coming through the window, someone who looked suspiciously like Jemima Jessop.

Don't be ridiculous, he thought to himself. *It's just nerves. You can do this, Masher. You HAVE to.*

On the other side of the room, Jemima wished she wasn't there either. She hated the idea of Masher stealing something in order to frame her and her family, and she certainly detested the fact that she had to apprehend him when he wasn't wearing any trousers. In fact, the sight of his legs appalled her so greatly that the first thing she did was remove his jeans from the window latch and throw them at him, watching the legs wrap around his ears like a crazed octopus, albeit one with only two legs.

The shock of the attack threw Masher off-balance, his body flying forward and whacking the table the medal sat on.

'Those jeans are the only things you're leaving this room with,' Jemima told him, her voice calm, despite her nerves.

Masher might've had little dazed denim squids swimming

before his eyes, but he still recognised the girl enough to curse her presence. This was the last thing he needed. Especially because he knew that when she spoke, he didn't have the brain capacity to duel with her. Not tonight.

'Leave me alone, circus freak. This has got nothing to do with you.' Not exactly poetic or even vaguely correct, but he hoped it would get the message across.

'I think we both know that's not true, don't we? Just in the same way we both know you don't want to steal that medal. 'Cos it is the medal you've come for, isn't it, Masher? Let me guess, you've come to steal it, and once you've stolen it, you're going to hide it with all the other stuff that's gone missing.'

Masher felt heat rise in his cheeks. Why didn't he just deny it? Tell her she was wrong? But he didn't get a chance, as Jemima went on.

'So let me think, where's the most incriminating place you could stash all the loot, to make it look like it was us Jessops who nicked it?'

She stepped slowly around the room, scratching her chin, as if the answers were hidden in the shadows.

'I've got it! Twinkles's cage, right? Go on, deny it!'

Masher's mouth flopped open, like his jaw had turned to

blancmange.

He couldn't deny her claims. His brain flatly refused, due to panic. He managed to let out a snail trail of dribble that wormed its way apologetically towards the floor.

'You know nothing,' he said eventually, wiping the corners of his mouth.

'Come on now. We both know that I know everything, or at the very least I know a lot more than you do.'

'You reckon?' Masher spat bullishly.

Bullies might not be bright, but they are rubbish at backing down.

'I know I do. For example, I know you don't want to steal that medal. I know you're only doing it to impress your dad.'

'That's garbage and you know it.' As if to prove it, Masher picked the medal up off the table defiantly and tried to shove it in his jeans pocket. Except he still wasn't wearing his jeans, and he realised that if he tried to shove it down his Y-fronts, the weight of the medal would pull his pants to the ground. He tossed it casually from hand to hand, like the world's rubbishest juggler.

'Look, Masher. I'm not here to fight you. I'm here because, well, I love it on Storey Street. It's exciting, you know, way more exciting than it looks. And to be honest, I just want to stay here.

For good. So I don't care why you're nicking that medal, whether it's because of your dad or just because you hate me. All I can say is, don't take it. Please?'

On hearing these words, Masher's moral radar went mental. How did she do this? She was their sworn enemy. Dad had said so. Her family wanted nothing but to get in their way. So why, when she spoke, was he constantly reminded of just how decent she was? Why didn't she behave like him or his dad?

He shut his eyes, trying to shake her face from his head. And somehow, it seemed to work, as there instead appeared his dad, his expression fierce and expectant. 'Milners Mash,' he whispered. 'It's what we do. We win at all costs. Don't let me down.'

Those words stirred something in Masher, reminding him like a jab to the ribs.

'I don't know what you're going on about,' Masher said, eyes opening. 'And even if I did, I still wouldn't care. So you'd better get out of my way, 'cos I'm going through that window any second now. And not you or nobody is going to stop me.'

At that moment, the sweating figure of Danny Christmas appeared in the room, slithering through the window with all the heroic qualities of a big-nosed slug.

'Ha!' laughed Masher, the sight of his old foe boosting his nastiness levels. 'I see the cavalry has arrived. What's he going to do, call down a miracle from above? Or has he got Santa waiting on the roof?'

'Turn yourself in,' Danny boomed, standing tall and copying a line from a rubbish cop movie. 'It's the only way.'

'You two need to turn it in,' Masher replied aggressively, determined to get out, though his brain screamed *ARGH! Get out of there, Masher, quickly, and take the medal with you. It's easier to disappoint these two than it is Dad.*

'I'm going now,' he said, giving them the chance to get out of the way.

Jemima didn't move. And Danny, spotting her resolve, didn't either.

'I said MOVE!' Masher roared.

The human barrier remained. It also replied: 'Please, Masher. Don't do this.' Jemima looked him in the eye, pleading.

'MOVE.'

'Please, Masher. Please. Don't.'

'I have to.'

'Says who?'

At this moment, it would've been the easiest thing in the

world for him to say, 'My dad.' But as he heard the words in his head, he realised how lame it sounded, how cowardly it made him look. And he wasn't a coward, he wasn't. He was Masher Milner. And he had to prove it.

'I say so!' he yelled, and ploughed forward, knocking Danny and Jemima over without raising a finger. Down they fell, powerless, as Masher flung his jeans over his shoulder, opened the big window and stepped onto the window ledge.

Jemima looked up in horror. He was getting away with it. Her plan had failed. What on earth was going to happen next?

Reader, there's only one way to find out . . .

(Read the next page, dumbo.)

Hanging by a Thread ... or Was It His Pants?

Masher didn't want to look back. The expression on Jemima's face was too pained and confusing for him to see again. But, saying that, he didn't want to look down either, as it reminded him how high up he was. It was bad enough that he had no jeans on, he also had no safety rope either. Heart pounding, palms sweating and conscience crumbling, Masher knew he had no option except to slide down that drainpipe as quickly as possible, to give Dad the medal and let him do what he wanted with it. At least that way, he wouldn't be a disappointment, and maybe, once Jemima had been moved on, he'd forget about her, and be able to get back to his old, simpler ways.

With the medal between his teeth, Masher checked the coast was clear, before wrapping his mitts around the pipe. As he rested his full weight upon it, he heard a groan from above (as if the pipe were saying, 'Are you kidding me? Again??') and

watched in terror
as the clasp that
fastened the tube
to the wall gave way,
causing the pipe to
lurch from the house
at a perilous forty-five
degree angle.

Masher wanted to
scream; the medal in his mouth
was the only thing that stopped him.
All he could manage was a throaty groan that
sounded like the arrival of a zombie apocalypse.

'What was that?' asked Danny from the bedroom.

'Sounded like the arrival of a zombie apocalypse,' replied Jemima. 'Well, that, or a drainpipe lurching from the house at a perilous forty-five degree angle, with Masher clinging to it.'

They both dashed to the window, horrified to see that Jemima was fifty per cent right.

'Oh, my lord,' Danny yelled. 'Now what?'

Jemima was already moving. With a leap she was

through the window, and with a spring she was back on the telephone wire, dancing towards the stricken Masher.

'Hold on!' she yelled. Not that Masher had many other options.

Within seconds she was in line with him, but frustratingly still out of reach.

With no thought for her own safety, she bent her knees, balance never wavering, until she was lying on the wire.

Extending her arm, she yelled,

'Grab onto me!'

Masher shook his head.

'I said HOLD ON!'

Slowly, Masher released one arm from the pipe, but instead of reaching for Jemima, he took the medal from his mouth and offered it to her.

'I don't want the medal!' she shouted. 'I don't give a monkey's about that. Drop it or throw it, just give me your arm.'

What followed was the weirdest, high-risk dance imaginable, as Masher continued to thrust the medal in Jemima's direction, only for her to refuse it. Eventually, with every bit of focus he had, Masher hurled it back towards the house, causing Danny to duck, in order to avoid wearing it like a monocle. It glided through the window, and landed, harmlessly, on the bed.

Then, and only then, did Masher slowly reach his arm out to Jemima.

'Can you really do this?' he cried. 'You are a . . .'

'What? A girl? Yeah, I am, but I'm also a circus freak girl, which makes me stronger than you'll ever be. So give me your hand and let's get on with it, shall we?'

Closing his eyes, hoping the drainpipe would hold, Masher thrust his arm skywards, and felt Jemima's hand take his. Her fingers were soft, but her grip wasn't. Nor were her biceps. Jemima hoisted Masher towards the telephone wire, closer and closer to relative safety. But just as the peril seemed to be averted, Masher inexplicably panicked. Maybe an image of his fuming dad flashed into his brain, maybe the seriousness of his crime had finally registered, or maybe it was the sight of a cocky pigeon gliding cockily in front of him, reminding him his feet were nowhere near the ground. Whatever was responsible, it was enough to see Masher thrashing at the wire, wobbling it so severely that even Jemima failed to balance, her body veering from side to side.

'Let go of me or you'll fall too!' Masher yelled.

Jemima shook her head and gritted her teeth.

'I said let GO!' Masher might have been a thug, but he didn't want to be responsible for two people falling to the ground.

With a mighty flail of his arm, he shook Jemima's grasp from his, and felt his body weight fall backwards, the leaning drainpipe zooming back into view.

His brain was scrambled by panic (and his legs cold without his jeans), but Masher knew this was his last chance, and he lunged towards the pipe, wrapping his arms and legs around it like a limpet with abandonment issues.

Above, Jemima breathed a sigh of relief, though only momentarily, because the pipe began to groan again under the pressure of Masher's weight, and it pulled further away from the wall.

'WAAAAAAAAAH!' Masher squealed. He hadn't banked on the bravery of one Danny Christmas, though, still perched on the bedroom window ledge.

Seeing the top of the drainpipe race past, Danny made a grab for it, and almost wished he hadn't, when it nearly dragged him into thin air too. But Christmas Junior was made of surprisingly stern stuff. With his right hand gripping the open window like an anchor, he heaved upon the drainpipe with his left, somehow managing to stop it capsizing further towards the ground.

'That's it, Danny,' called Jemima. 'Hold on. I'm coming.'

'Hurry!' he screamed in reply. 'I think my arm is coming out of its socket!'

Masher didn't say anything intelligible. He had his eyes closed and was making a noise that sounded like a mixture of a prayer and a scream. Let's call it a pream, shall we?

So, as Masher preamed with all his might, Jemima dashed across the telephone wire and jumped onto the window ledge, just as the force of the drainpipe was becoming too much for Danny to hold. Clamping her arms around his waist, Jemima felt the pipe stop once more. Digging her heels in, she then leaned back and, imploring Danny to use whatever strength he had left, together they slowly pulled Masher and the pipe back into an upright position, so that the bully was five metres above them, almost at roof level.

'You're going to have to shimmy down,' she shouted up at him.

'I can't.'

'Don't be such a plonker,' Jemima shouted. 'We can't hold on for ever. Come on, before you end up wearing that rose bush in the garden.'

Masher looked down. He might have been a long way from the ground, but he could still see how sharp the thorns were on the bush. With fear gnawing at his belly, he edged himself down the pole, until Jemima could yank him to safety.

'I don't want to die!' he wept, as she forced him through the window and back into the bedroom.

'Er . . . I think you'll be fine,' Jemima said. 'At the moment the only risk of death comes from us all drowning in your tears.'

Masher lifted his head and looked at his saviour through bloodshot eyes.

'Why did you do that?' he asked, with an almighty sniff.

'What, stop you from becoming garden fertiliser? I would've thought that was obvious.'

'I've been nothing but horrible to you since the second you arrived. I threw that mud pie at you . . .'

'I remember.'

'Then I cheated in that race, pushed you to the ground and hurt your knee.'

'I remember that too.'

'And there was the beast Dad made . . . and now this!'

'I know, I know. I was there, remember? And it's OK. You were just . . .' She tried to think of the right word. A word that wouldn't hurt him any more than he was already.

'UNHAPPY!' Danny interrupted, finally understanding. 'You were just unhappy!' And he patted Masher tentatively on the shoulder, in the way you'd pat a huge crying dog that might still bite your arm off.

But Masher didn't bite. He didn't bark. He didn't even growl.

Jemima looked at Danny, and Danny looked at Jemima. This was a Masher they didn't recognise.

They didn't have a clue what would happen next.

24.

Never Can Say Goodbye

Jemima watched Masher slump nervously towards his front door.

'Do you think he'll be OK?' she asked Danny.

'Don't know. At least he's got his jeans back on. Not that his dad will care. Only thing he's bothered about is framing you.'

Jemima nodded sadly, remembering the expression on Masher's face after they'd pulled him to safety. She'd never seen anyone so scared or confused in her life.

She'd listened as he slumped on the bed. 'He's going to kill me,' Masher repeated, again and again.

Jemima tried to reason with him, calm him down. 'You almost managed to do that without your dad's help,' she said, but Masher didn't see the funny side.

'This was my chance,' he cried. 'To be just like him. Show him I'm not a wimp.'

'A wimp?!' Jemima spluttered. 'We could call you a lot of

names, Masher, most of them beginning with "W". "Wally" and "wazzock" spring to mind immediately, but "wimp" isn't one of them, believe me.'

'I'm not tough like he is,' Masher said. 'Not really. I could try and Mash everything in sight. Every plant, every person, every . . .'

'Potato?' Danny suggested.

'But it would never be enough. I'd never do it as quick or as well as he can. I must be the biggest disappointment imaginable.'

'So why even try to impress him?' Jemima said calmly. 'Just be different. You don't have to do things his way.'

Masher stared at her intently, cogs turning. *Wow,* thought Danny, *she's getting through to him, he's going to see the light.*

On he stared, eyes widening as he parted his lips to speak. Here it came, the BIG apology for all the agony he'd inflicted over the last ten years.

'That,' Masher started, his voice low and slow, '. . . is the most RIDICULOUS THING I HAVE EVER HEARD IN MY LIFE!! You've met him. If I ever tried to grow up different to him, he'd make my life a misery. He'd disown me. That or string me up from the nearest lamp post!'

'Really? Well, that sounds familiar, doesn't it? Sounds exactly like what happened ten minutes ago, doesn't it? And it can't be any worse than that, can it? Really?'

Masher deflated quicker than a balloon with a gunshot wound. He had no answer for them. But he couldn't apologise either. He didn't know how to. His dad had never taught him that.

Instead, Jemima took the lead, walking over to the bed and fetching the medal, which she put gently in his bulbous right fist.

'Here you go,' she said. 'This is what you came for. Do what you want with it. It's up to you.'

Danny couldn't believe what he was seeing. Why did Jemima always do the opposite of what any normal person would do? They'd just saved Masher from rearranging his body into a pool of pus and she was going to let him walk out of there with everything he came for? Unbelievable.

But Masher didn't leave. He didn't move. Instead, he stood and stared at his fist, like it contained the greatest secret ever told.

Then, slowly, slowly, he started to walk towards the door.

Jemima breathed deeply as her brain yelled conflicting things at her.

Stop him! it bawled, as well as, *Let him make his own mind up!*

She wanted to scream, she wanted to grab him, but something deep down in her shoes stopped her.

And you know what? She was right. For, as Masher passed

the bedside table, he palmed the medal back into place, then stopped and looked back. 'I'm leaving by the back door. I suggest you do the same. Tell anyone about what went on here and I'll Mash every single bone in your bodies.'

And that was it, he was gone, our intrepid heroes following at a distance, until his front door slammed, the sound echoing the length of Storey Street.

'Blimey,' sighed Danny, exhaustion replacing adrenalin. 'We only bloomin' well did it.'

'We did,' replied Jemima, her relief not as evident as his.

'We should check Twinkles's cage. I bet Maurice has already put half the stolen stuff in there. He might not have the medal, but he could still call the police and dump you in it.'

But Jemima didn't want his help.

'It'll be fine,' she said. 'I'll sort it out.'

'Cheer up!' Danny said. 'Don't you see what this means? It'll keep your mum and dad sweet about this place. They'll be happy to stay, we can still use your back garden, PLUS we can stop the Milners taking over the street. Everyone's a winner!'

Jemima painted on the finest smile she could muster. She liked loads of things about Danny Christmas. He was the most open and generous person she'd met in all her years on the road, but he still didn't quite get it. Jemima knew they'd stopped the Milners for now, but how long until the next plan got hatched, and how monstrous would that one be?

She tried to think about how to explain this, but Danny was so high on their adventure she didn't have the heart to bring him crashing down.

'We won't let them buy The House That Was Stolen, Danny, I promise. You have my word.'

'Brilliant,' Danny smiled. He knew Jemima wouldn't fail him. 'So I'll see you tomorrow. I'll call for you on the way to school.'

Jemima didn't answer. Not directly anyway. Instead she stepped forward and hugged him, making his nose so red it made Rudolph's look pale.

'You're lovely, Danny Christmas. Don't forget that.'

'Er . . . OK. Won't do. Not between now and eight o'clock tomorrow anyway.' He looked at his watch. 'I'd better get inside.

My dad'll crucify me if he finds me here at this time.'

Jemima dissolved into giggles. 'With his job, you numbnut, I find that seriously unlikely.'

Cue laughter, from both of them.

'See you in the morning,' Danny said.

'Laters,' Jemima replied, and she waited until Danny had crept stealthily through his door. Then, after casting an eye up Storey Street, lingering the longest on Milner Mansions, she sighed, and went inside too.

25. Wake Up, It's a Beautiful Morning . . .

Grey was the colour. Clouds hung over Storey Street like a drab woollen blanket. They'd infiltrated Milner Mansions too, surrounding Masher as he sat on his bed, legs hugged to his chest. He'd been in that position for hours after giving up on sleep, his dad's voice still booming in his ears.

'What do you mean, you haven't got the medal?' Maurice had raged.

It was a rage Masher had expected, but still hadn't enjoyed. He'd felt Dad's anger coming off him and he'd had no idea what to say next. Should he lie? Or tell the truth?

'I tried, Dad, didn't I? Climbed the drainpipe, like you said, and climbed through the window, but then—'

'Then what? Was the medal not there? Did someone disturb you?'

Masher had latched on to Dad's last question.

'Yes, that's it. Someone else was in the house. A couple of people.' Technically, it wasn't a lie, but it still hadn't pleased Dad.

'Then you should've grabbed the medal before getting out. You're a Milner, for goodness' sake, and Milners always get the job done!'

Maurice had marched to the window, sending Masher into panic. What if Jemima and Danny were still outside and Dad worked it all out? He'd go mental if he knew his own flesh and blood had been foiled by a circus girl and a Christmas elf.

'The Tippses' car is back outside their house,' he'd fumed, allowing Masher to breathe again. 'It must've been them coming home. Honestly, Masher, I give you one little job and you go and let me down. I sometimes wonder if you really want to be a Milner at all!'

Masher hadn't known how to answer. How could Dad call breaking into someone's house little? Or doubt his loyalty?

But Maurice hadn't been in the mood for excuses or explanations.

'The medal was the final part of the jigsaw, the thing to send the neighbours into overdrive, but I reckon we've still got enough junk in the shed to have the Jessops and their tin can towed away. So if you want to restore my belief in you, if you want me to believe that you could possibly be my son after all, you'll play along out there and be the Masher I've brought you up to be. Now get up to your room and start practising. First thing in the morning, I'll call the police and you'd better be ready.'

With a heavy heart, and an even heavier cloud resting on his shoulders, Masher had climbed the wooden hill to Bedfordshire.

Nine hours (and zero minutes of sleep) later, Masher slumped down the stairs to find Dad ending a phone call.

'Chief Waggle and his boys in blue are on the way,' he said, without once looking at Masher. 'So get behind me and back me up. No weakness, no surrender. And remember who you are.' Throwing his smartest suit jacket over his shoulders like a matador's cape, Maurice led his son through the door and prepared himself for the kill.

Masher wasn't feeling quite so bullish. He'd fretted all night long.

What should he do?

Jemima had seen through their plan, and he couldn't believe she was going to leave all the stolen stuff in Twinkles's cage. But at the same time, he didn't have the bravery to own up to Dad. And now? Well now it was too late. All he could do was play dumb to whatever happened next.

The sight that greeted him next door, though, well, dear reader, there's no easy way to sugar the pill. It may break your heart. It certainly did mine.

Because Masher's eyes weren't greeted by a white picket fence, impeccable lawn and shining silver caravan. All he could see was a gap where a house should sit, plus a shabby old settee, a TV and a lamp.

'What . . . ?' Masher mouthed, pushing his way to the front of a gathering crowd, where he spotted a forlorn Danny Christmas.

'They can't have. They wouldn't. Would they?' The red-nosed wonder was inconsolable, whereas Masher was simply bemused. Why on earth would the Jessops do a bunk when there was no reason to? Jemima held all the cards, why was she throwing them away? He didn't know whether to feel the most incredible relief or overwhelming shame.

But there was no way of dressing up the truth. No frilly bow or pretty dress that could make it more palatable. The Jessops had gone. It was as if they'd never been there in the first place. They'd left the House That Was Stolen exactly as they'd found it.

Confusion reigned. Elliot Tipps hunted for his football pitch, Laszlo Di Bosco looked under the settee for the plasma screen telly. Neither found what they were looking for, and both of them howled in disbelief.

Danny Christmas was after something else though – the truth – and he scoured the crowd for it, before his gaze landed on the mayor, Stanley Albertson, who was stepping out of a police car with Inspector Waggle and three of his burliest police officers.

'Mr Albertson, Mr Albertson,' Danny said, pulling on his chain of office. 'Did you see what happened here? Did you see where they went?'

The big man shook his ruddy, wobbling cheeks. 'I didn't, son.'

'You have to help us find them. Call the SAS or something!'

'And say what? They're not missing. They lived in a caravan, and caravans have wheels for a reason.'

Danny was crestfallen. 'So this means the Milners can build on the land after all?'

'It does, son. No one else has come forward and the land is

empty, so we've no choice but to accept their offer.'

A yelp of delight leaped from Maurice Milner's mouth. Masher wanted to feel relief, but felt more like burping nauseously.

'I'll buy it instead!!' blurted Danny, knowing he didn't have so much as a bean in his pocket, but so desperate he'd have said anything at that moment in time. He'd have announced he was a unicorn called Daphne if it managed to stop the Milners' horrible plan.

'I think we all know that's not going to happen,' Maurice beamed. 'It looks like our travelling friends have finally done the right thing. They've left a bit of mess, but don't worry, it's nothing my builders can't tidy up, and they can be here in five minutes flat.'

Danny looked to Masher, imploring him silently to step in and do something. To remember what happened last night. Repay the debt he owed.

Masher wet his lips, as if ready to speak, but as he raised his eyes to the towering figure of his dad, who was already on the phone to his troops, his shoulders and spirit sagged powerlessly to the floor. He couldn't do it. Couldn't ask or beg Dad not to go on. Couldn't tell him they didn't have to win. Not this way.

The next few minutes were a blur. Danny raced around the crowd begging anyone to throw him a lifeline, but no one had so much as a rubber duck, never mind a rubber ring. Even his dear dad, usually so good in a crisis, had nothing to offer. Well, nothing except prayer anyway.

All Danny could do was sit dejectedly on the sofa of The House That Was Stolen and listen as the diggers, lorries and cement mixers rumbled into earshot. He'd lost everything: his hopes, his new best friend, and soon they'd lose the settee and the rest of the house too. All those years and memories of hanging out, resigned to ancient history. It just wasn't fair!

Two minutes later and a stream of builders had infested the site, measuring, pondering and drinking tea, while two burly bricklayers hoisted the settee into the air, not bothering to tip Danny off it first.

'Put me down!!' he yelled tearfully. 'That's our house you're wrecking. It isn't theirs, it never will be.'

Masher watched, stomach churning, brain whirring, as Dad marshalled the builders gleefully. Danny looked on in horror as a builder kneeled and prepared to lay the first brick that would turn his life in to a living coffin.

Then, just as the brick was about to make contact with the soil, the air was punctured by a strange sound. A sound not usually connected with a building site, but with a circus ring: the sound of a comedy horn.

PARP! It sounded. *PAAARRRRRRP!*

Now I love a good parp as much as the next man, and the next man is a man who is fart-gag mad, but what on earth was it doing here? And now?

The builders stopped, downed tools and looked behind them to see a clown, dressed in full regulation circus gear and driving a comedy trike with a horn attached to the handlebars. Masher wondered if his sleep-deprived brain was playing games with him.

Arriving on the pavement by the builders, the clown let off one last *PARP*, so loud that it seemed to come accompanied with an eggy smell.

'Hello, troops.' He beamed. 'Saul McShiftyson here, attorney-at-law. Not my usual gig this, but the clients are paying so well, I couldn't turn down the demand that I deliver this in fancy dress. I'm looking for a . . .' And, pulling a large brown envelope from his inside pocket, he read, 'Master Danny Christmas. Anyone here matching that unusual and actually rather funny name? I mean, imagine if his dad was a vicar? That'd make him Father Christmas!'

A few of the builders laughed, but not Danny, who leapt off the settee and dashed to the clown's side.

'That's me,' he shouted. 'What is it? What have you got?'

'See for yourself,' the clown answered. 'If you want me to explain it too, that'll cost you extra, and to be honest I'd rather just get home. These clown shoes are killing me.' He handed Danny the bulging envelope, before pulling off his red nose, jumping back on the bike and cycling away. He must've been off-duty by then, as he didn't parp his horn as he left. Not even once. The spoilsport.

This left Danny moving away from a curious-looking Masher and tearing at the envelope to reveal a thick wedge of official-looking papers, which contained words that made absolutely no sense, like 'forthwith', 'henceforth' and 'fartynostril'. (OK, I made that last one up.)

Anyway, the documents looked so boring and unimportant that Masher and his dad relaxed slightly, while the builders continued to lay bricks, dig trenches and shout for more tea, even if their mugs were still sloshing with the stuff.

But as Danny turned over the seventeenth page of the document, a note fell to the floor, written in friendly handwriting, using words that weren't pure gobbledygook.

Without anyone else seeing, Danny picked it up, his eyes tearing hungrily across the page.

Dear Danny,

I'm sorry I'm not here to tell you this in person, but Mum and Dad decided it was best that we leave straightaway.

None of us want to live somewhere that we aren't universally wanted. Life's too short. Besides, we'll find somewhere, and when we do, you can come and visit!

Danny stopped reading, his eyes misting. He didn't want to visit. He'd wanted them to stay!

But don't be getting all emotional about it, Danny Christmas, because that is where the bad news stops. Everything else in this letter is good. Surprising, maybe, but good. I promise.

You see, that document full of words like 'forthwith', 'henceforth' and 'fartynostril' is really important, so don't throw it away or use it as loo roll. It's called a 'Deed of Transfer'. I know that still sounds boring, but bear with me. You see, The House That Was Stolen doesn't belong to no one. It belongs to us. The Jessops. I know, proper shoc king, eh?

My great-great-great-great-grandparents owned the land – they won it in a card game – but because they were circus folk and always on the road, they never built on it. Over the years, it's been passed down through many Jessop generations, and now it belongs to us. Or at least it did.

You see me, Mum, Dad and John-boy have talked about it, and because we're never going to live in it, we want to pass it on to people who are more deserving, people who aren't going to build a really rubbish mansion on it.

Masher heard a yelp of delight. It seemed to have burst out of Danny Christmas's mouth, but his big-nosed neighbour had recovered his poise and was absorbed again in the boring papers in front of him.

If only Masher could've seen just what those papers really said . . .

As The House That Was Stolen has always really belonged to the children of Storey Street, we've decided to give it to you properly. All of you. All you have to do is promise never to build on it, and to always ensure there is a TV, settee and lamp there at all times. Whatever else you do with it is up to you. It's yours to decide. To make the deal legally binding, every child who lives on the street has to sign the last page. There's a list of names there to help you.

So that's it. I hope this makes you grin. I hope it feels like all your Christmases have come at once . . . HA! See what I did there?

I'll miss you, Danny. A lot. But keep your eye out for unicycles. You never know who might pedal by.

Look after the house for me. And Masher too. He's all right, he is, despite how "unhappy" he gets.

Bye bye,

Your pal,

Jemima Jessop

Another yelp invaded Masher's ears. A yelp that everyone heard (even above the din of the cement mixers and constantly boiling kettles).

There was no doubt who the yelper was either, as there stood Danny Christmas, arm held high, still clutching the sheath of papers, his voice confident and defiant as he roared.

'OI! YOU LOT IN THE HELMETS. STOP RIGHT THERE! GET YOUR HANDS OFF OUR HOUSE!'

26.

Sign Your Name Across My Heart

Well, well, well, this news really did cause a stir.

Danny's words were met with a range of reactions: gasps, cheers, and a clunking, screeching noise From Masher's brain. *You have to be kidding me?* he said to himself, his head unable to comprehend yet another twist in the tale. Just when it seemed his dad was finally going to get his devious way . . .

He looked at his old man, who was already thundering through the crowd, smoke singeing the hair that grew in his earholes.

'Give me those papers,' he shouted, making grabby hands, only to be thwarted by Danny climbing on top of the

TV, before passing them safely to the mayor.

'It's all above board and official,' Stanley Albertson nodded reluctantly, feeling the fiery breath of Maurice on his neck. 'Though for the deal to go through, every child has to agree and sign. If one person refuses, the deal is null and void.'

This news didn't disturb Danny too much. I mean, there wasn't a kid who didn't love The House That Was Stolen. Who wouldn't want to put a stop to the Milners' plan?

Borrowing a pen from Stanley Albertson, Danny took up residence on the settee with the contract on his knee, and started to call the children of Storey Street up, one by one, to sign on the dotted line.

The first dozen names proved no problem, even when one or two needed to be called away from their breakfast or their beds. Danny's smile stretched wider every time the pen made contact with the paper.

On the names went:

Jake Biggs

Michael J Mouse

Kay Catt

Elliot Tipps

They didn't seem to be in alphabetical order, but that didn't bother Danny: within half an hour he had forty-seven signatures. There were only two left to gather.

Excitement in the crowd was rife. So was anxiety. Was this really about to happen?

Danny looked back to the paper, fist pumping the air when he saw that the penultimate name was his own. Hand shaking with excitement he scrawled on the sheet, eyes flicking down to the final name.

The name that would make the whole transaction official.

And that name was . . . ?

Oh no.

Danny's face drained of blood.

'M-M-Masher Milner,' Danny called out weakly, drawing a gasp from the crowd, and almost from Masher too.

How could Danny have not realised that Masher would have to sign too? How could he have forgotten that, although he was the worst bully in Seacross history, Masher was also still a kid?

The crowd parted for the bully to walk through. But Masher wasn't going anywhere. He stood, fists twitching, brain so desperately, desperately tired. What on earth did he do now?

'Ha ha ha! Oh, this is brilliant,' roared Maurice, who danced riotously in the crowd, taking the hugest delight in every child's misery. 'Here you all are, lording it up, thinking you're so superior. This just proves to everyone one of you worms that you will never, ever, get one over on the Milners.'

Maurice was so over-excited, he seemed to have forgotten that he was openly ridiculing a bunch of children, some as young as three. Every child he passed he wagged a finger in their face, or shook his bottom in defiance. Unsavoury wasn't the word for it, believe me.

'You're a loser,' he roared. 'You are too, and you, and you. You'll only ever be a shelf-stacker, you'll only clean toilets for a living. 'Cos WE are the powerful ones around here. You mark my words, this is just the beginning, because the next time a house goes up for sale on this street, we'll buy it. And the next one, and the one after that as well, until finally we'll own the whole lot. And there won't be anything any of you can do about it. 'Cos that's how powerful we are. Isn't that right, son?'

Masher still didn't move, though he did stare at his dad, who was standing directly between him and a fearful, tearful Danny.

'Let's go home and let these losers sob in private. It's time for a slap-up breakfast, I reckon.'

Right on cue, Masher started to walk in his dad's direction, fists still clenched. But as he reached him, a strange thing happened. He didn't alter his course and follow him home. He walked in a straight line, past his old man, and towards Danny, who by now was slumped, distraught, on the settee.

Danny felt Masher loom over him, his bulk blocking out the sun. He cowered. He knew from previous experience what to expect.

Masher's arm shot out. Danny flinched. The bully's arm stopped short of his face. Instead it hovered in mid-air as Masher spoke a single word.

'Pen,' he grunted.

'Pardon?' Danny really hoped he hadn't said 'pain'.

'I said "pen".'

Danny lifted his eyes to meet Masher's but they gave nothing away. No warmth, nothing.

Danny did as he was told, his hand shaking in the process.

Masher leaned over the document, while his dad leaned over his shoulder in turn.

'Masher?' Maurice spat. 'What are you doing?'

'Making a stand,' he answered.

'What, against me?'

Masher pressed down on the paper, hand scribbling, then

turned to face his dad. 'No, not against you. For me. I don't have to be like you. I've just realised that actually I can do things my way if I want.'

His words may have sounded confident, but inside, Masher was quivering. He couldn't believe he was saying this to his dad. And he couldn't believe how good it felt either.

Maurice looked like the top of his head was about to blow clean off.

'Do you know what message you're sending out here?' he hissed. 'That you're weak. That WE are weak.'

Masher shrugged, a smile playing softly on his lips. 'So what? Maybe sometimes we don't have to Mash everything in sight.'

'Don't you know who you are, boy? Don't you know what that means?'

'I thought I knew the answers to both those questions, Dad,' Masher said. 'But it turns out that I didn't. Not until now.'

And he strode purposefully past Maurice, past the residents of Storey Street, who parted slowly, a sea of arms reaching forward one by one to pat Masher on the back. Each pat made Masher feel taller, so much so that as he reached his front gate he felt like a skyscraper. So tall, that as he approached their shed, he had an idea.

Purposefully, before he could change his mind, Masher walked to its door.

Maurice started to hyperventilate. 'Masher? Son! What are you doing?'

'What I should've done days ago,' he answered from inside the shed as he whipped the tarpaulin aside.

Then with great bravery, he pulled a doorknocker from the bottom of the pile of loot, starting an avalanche that rumbled and tumbled, filling their yard with stolen stuff.

'Hey!' yelled Jack Boo. 'That's our letterbox!'

'And our front gate!' shouted Timmy Bentone.

Maurice Milner looked like a man who'd just realised he was allergic to prison food.

'Wait,' he gasped. 'I can explain. It's all some terrible mistake . . .' But from the corner of his eye he spotted Police Inspector Waggle and his boys in blue, walking towards him, handcuffs primed.

'Waggle, please, let's talk. There must be an agreement we can reach. I've got a lovely little semi-detached on our books, make a smashing place for you and your fam—'

But the officers weren't interested in a deal on a new home for themselves. All they wanted was to give Maurice a new residence. The sort with bars and a mighty big lock on the doors.

Maurice turned and sped through the crowd, who despite their best efforts, couldn't hold him. Up the street Maurice tore, his voice fading gradually as he screamed 'Masher! Maaasshheeeeer! Help meeeeeeeee . . .'

But Masher didn't want to help. In fact he'd already gone inside, closing the door with a gentle click, leaving the adults to slowly, slowly disperse and go about their business.

Only the kids remained, as they so often did, at The House That Was Stolen.

Danny Christmas sat on the settee and stared at the papers in his hand as his friends gathered around him.

He still couldn't believe what had just happened.

He wanted it all to be true. That Masher had defied his dad, that the house did indeed belong to every kid on Storey Street. But he couldn't believe it was so. There had to be a catch.

Hesitantly, he looked down at the piece of paper in front of him and checked that Masher really had signed his name, not just scrawled 'Up yours, Rudolph' or something equally witty.

Focusing his eyes, he panicked at first, when he didn't see 'Masher' written at the start; there was no rounded hump of the letter 'M'. Only the circle and stick of a crudely scrawled 'Q'.

Danny smiled. Masher had meant everything he said to his dad. This document proved it in black and white.

There was his name. The name that gifted The House That Was Stolen back to the kids.

The name was Milner.

Quentin Milner.

27. This Is the End, Beautiful Friend

Just another normal Sunday on Storey Street.

Cars were being washed, shopping unpacked, window frames painted.

A front door opened to reveal two figures: an elderly, stooped old lady, and her hulking grandson, all shaved head and steel toecapped boots.

The boy picked the post up from the mat, passing bills to his grandma, before spotting a postcard from Brazil complete with a message in familiar handwriting.

'Another one from Dad,' the boy said, no hint of emotion in his voice, though he did wonder how long it would be until the police finally tracked him down.

'Shall I put it with all the others?' the old lady said.

The boy nodded. The bin was the best place for it.

Buttoning up his denim jacket, the boy said goodbye to his

grandma and looked over at The House That Was Stolen, where it was business as usual.

Polly Stagger, Anaya Shan and Eleanor Pulse were sitting on the settee debating the merits of Justin Bieber's new single (it was another blissfully brief conversation), while next to them tutted Laszlo Di Bosco, who was trying to watch something on the telly, despite it having never worked due to a complete lack of electricity.

Behind them, a game of footie had broken out, the Story Street Trophy the prize on offer.

The two teams were lead by Elliot Tipps (son of legendary Seacross Tigers goalkeeper, Tony Tipps) and Danny Christmas (son of legendary Seacross vicar, Father Christmas . . . titter, chortle, guffaw).

It was a tense game, nil-nil, with only two minutes left to play, when Tipps made a surging run. Dancing past the opposition, he closed in on the goal. There was only Danny Christmas to beat, and, well, he was no shot-stopper. History showed that, time and time again. As keepers went, he was utter bobbins.

Not wanting to take risks, though, Tipps pulled back his bazooka of a left boot and let fly with a real screamer.

But Danny Christmas was not afraid. He'd learned lately that there was nothing, NOTHING, he couldn't do, not if he stayed calm.

Keeping his eyes on the path of the ball, he threw himself to the left, and with amazing strength and athleticism, palmed the ball against the bar.

The crowd. Went. Wild.

Well, they would've done if there had been one, but in Danny's head at least, the whole stadium rose as one to applaud him.

The ball bounced towards the road and into the path of an oncoming pedestrian, who trapped the ball with his huge boot.

Danny's eyes travelled up from the boot, past the leg and body until it reached the face of Quentin Milner.

Danny gulped. That would be the end of their ball. The bully had burst plenty over the years, all of them intentionally.

'Kick it back for us, will you?' Danny shouted, with a hopeful smile.

There was a pause. Tension thickened like gravy in a sticky roasting pan.

The ball rested in Quentin's hands. He squeezed it, testing its strength. Then, without warning, his right boot pulled itself slowly back, and with an accurate whack, sent the ball spinning straight into Danny's arms.

'Thanks,' Danny yelled, and turned back to the match. But before he resumed play, he stopped, and turned back in Quentin's direction.

'Want to join in?' he shouted. 'It's nil-nil. One minute to play, and we could do with a bit of muscle up front.'

Quentin shook his head. 'Nah.'

Danny shrugged. 'Another day then?'

'Maybe,' Quentin answered, before turning away. 'Definitely maybe.'

And on he walked, his boots stomping out an impressive echo; a smile chiselling its way across his usually stony face.

The End(ish)

THE
AMAZING
JESSOPS

WITNESS
MASHER
HUMAN
VOLCANO
EXPLOSIVE!

MAURICE'S
SLEIGHT OF HAND
TRICKS
TRICKS
WINNER TAKES ALL

Acknowledgements...

Huge thanks to everyone at Hachette Children's Group, especially Fritha, Steph, Susan, Jen, Jennie and especially especially to Helen Thomas, whose kindness, care and listening skills are unparalleled.

Huge thanks also to Sara Ogilvie, whose illustrations continue to make me smile every time I see them.

Much love to Nina, Jenny, Jo and Fiona too, for believing in me, Masher and Co.

Thank you also to Jodie and Emily at UA for looking after me so regally.

Finally, as always, I owe the most thanks and love to my family: Laura, Albie, Elsie and Stanley. I don't have the words, so I'm not going to even try...

Hebden Bridge,
July, 2016

Don't miss the other Storey Street novels!

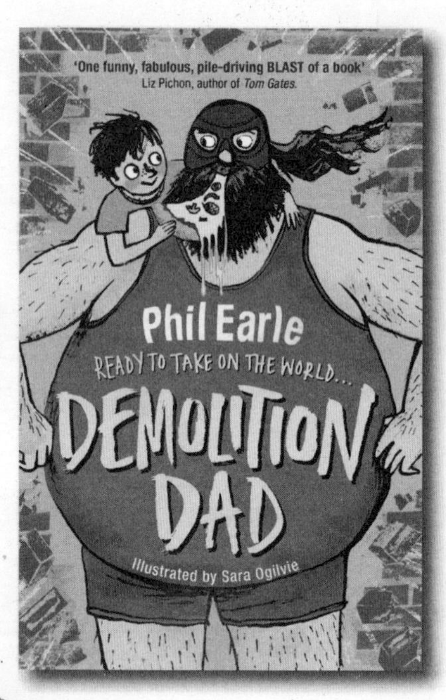